What secrets lie
Tsarichina Hole?

MW01223498

Dane Maddock and Bones Bonebrake to solve one of the
strangest mysteries of the Twentieth Century.

Dane and Bones have traveled to Sofia, Bulgaria to help
their friend Max Riddle shoot a new documentary
television show about the Tsarichina Hole, a shaft
excavated by the Bulgarian military in the early 1990s, on
the advice of a psychic remote viewer, and then abruptly
sealed for no apparent reason.

Riddle has found a back door into the excavation, known
to many as "Bulgaria's Area 51," and asks Dane and Bones
to help him explore the passage to nowhere. Their
discovery of a prized relic belonging to a famed Bulgarian
conqueror touches off a search for an even greater
treasure, and threatens to expose a secret that someone is
willing to kill to preserve.

Praise for David Wood and Sean Ellis!

"Dane and Bones. Together they're unstoppable. Rip
roaring action from start to finish. Wit and humor
throughout. Just one question - how soon until the next
one? Because I can't wait."-Graham Brown, author of
Shadows of the Midnight Sun

"What an adventure! A great read that provides lots of
action, and thoughtful insight as well, into strange realms
that are sometimes best left unexplored." -Paul
Kemprecos, author of *the NUMA Files*

DESTINATION: SOFIA
A DANE MADDOCK ADVENTURE

DAVID WOOD
SEAN ELLIS

BOOKS and SERIES by DAVID WOOD

The Dane Maddock Adventures
Blue Descent
Dourado
Cibola
Quest
Icefall
Buccaneer
Atlantis
Ark
Xibalba
Loch
Solomon Key
Contest

Dane and Bones Origins
Freedom
Hell Ship
Splashdown
Dead Ice
Liberty
Electra
Amber
Justice
Treasure of the Dead
Bloodstorm

Adventures from the Dane Maddock Universe
Destination-Rio
Destination-Luxor
Destination-Sofia
Berserk

Maug
The Elementals
Cavern
Devil's Face
Herald
Brainwash
The Tomb
Shasta (forthcoming)

Jade Ihara Adventures (with Sean Ellis)
Oracle
Changeling
Exile

Bones Bonebrake Adventures
Primitive
The Book of Bones
Skin and Bones
Venom

Jake Crowley Adventures (with Alan Baxter)
Blood Codex
Anubis Key
Revenant

Brock Stone Adventures
Arena of Souls
Track of the Beast (forthcoming)

Myrmidon Files (with Sean Ellis)
Destiny
Mystic

Sam Aston Investigations (with Alan Baxter)
Primordial
Overlord

Stand-Alone Novels
Into the Woods (with David S. Wood)
Callsign: Queen (with Jeremy Robinson)
Dark Rite (with Alan Baxter)

David Wood writing as David Debord

The Absent Gods Trilogy
The Silver Serpent
Keeper of the Mists
The Gates of Iron

The Impostor Prince (with Ryan A. Span)
Neptune's Key
The Zombie-Driven Life
You Suck

BOOKS and SERIES by SEAN ELLIS

The Nick Kismet Adventures
The Shroud of Heaven
Into the Black
The Devil You Know (Novella)
Fortune Favors

The Adventures of Dodge Dalton
In the Shadow of Falcon's Wings

At the Outpost of Fate
On the High Road to Oblivion
Against the Fall of Eternal Night (with Kerry Frey)

The Mira Raiden Adventures
Ascendant
Descendant

Magic Mirror
The Sea Wraiths and Other Tales
Camp Zero
WarGod (with Steven Savile)

(with Jeremy Robinson)
Prime
Savage
Cannibal
Empire
Herculean
Helios
Flood Rising
Callsign: King (novella)
Callsign: King—Underworld (novella)
Callsign: King—Blackout (novella)

(with David Wood)
Hell Ship
Oracle
Changeling
Exile
Destiny
Mystic
Outpost

Arcanum
Magus
Destination-Rio
Destination-Luxo
r

PROLOGUE

The villagers called him the Wolf, conferring upon him the esteemed title of *Voivode*, a term reserved for military commanders.

Both name and title were well-deserved.

He led a pack of fierce hunters, who ranged across the Balkan Mountains, from the Black Sea to the White, and like wolves, they did not hunt lions—the Pasha and his Janissaries—but instead chose to fall upon fat, defenseless cows—merchant caravans, heavily laden with the fruits of Bulgarian labor, destined for Constantinople. Yes, he was the wolf at the head of the pack, but he survived where others who had chosen to oppose the Turks failed, because he was more like a cunning fox, able to disappear into the very rocks when lions drew near. He could do this because he did not rest in the homes of the villagers he fought for. No, he lived in the hills, and under them. The Balkans were shot through with caves and tunnels, and while no man could know all of them, he knew more than most.

Soon, he would know of one more.

He had only heard rumors of the existence of this system of tunnels, but after an earthquake that had left most of the city in ruins, the Ottoman forces had withdrawn, giving him an unexpected opportunity to see if there was any truth to the rumors.

It was no surprise that these passageways had remained unexplored. There was barely enough room to crawl on his belly, pushing his little oil lamp ahead of him as he went. The air was unpleasantly hot, making it difficult to breathe. The passages themselves were a maze, and as he went deeper into it, the flame from his lamp began to burn a dull orange that provided scant illumination. At the first intersection he encountered, he had chosen to turn left, and then spent hours navigating a warren of passages with so many intersections that, had he not taken care to mark his route carefully, he would have become hopelessly lost. None of the passages led anywhere, though in several instances, he found heaps of loose earth where the roof had caved in. Perhaps an exit lay beyond those obstacles. If he did not find another way out, he would come back with tools and dig through.

He returned the next night to explore the middle passage, and this time made an astonishing discovery. After a few switchbacks, he discovered a side passage that appeared to have been sealed off intentionally behind a brick wall. That wall had collapsed, probably as a result of the earthquake. Instead of blocking his way, the quake had opened a path that would otherwise have escaped his notice. He cleared away the rubble and crawled into this new passage.

There were no turns, but soon the passage began to slope downward. This gave the Wolf pause. He was looking for a way out; he did not want to go deeper into the earth. Still, someone had sealed this passage off for a reason, and he wanted to know what it was. With his lamp held up in one hand, he scuttled forward on his belly until at last the passage flattened out and he emerged into a larger chamber. What he saw there so surprised him that he jerked the hand holding the lamp and accidentally doused the wick in oil, plunging him into utter darkness.

As he fumbled in his satchel for the metal can of matches, he wondered if his eyes had been playing tricks on him.

"Please God," he whispered into the darkness. "Please, let it be real."

His trembling fingers found a match, felt the bulb of sulfur and white phosphorus at the tip. He struck it and quickly held it up as the flare of light filled the darkness and was reflected back a million times over.

His eyes had not deceived him. God had heard his prayer.

Everywhere he looked, there was gold.

1

Uriah "Bones" Bonebrake unfolded himself from the shotgun seat of the beige Fiat 500L, and stretched his long limbs. At just a hair over six-feet-five-inches tall, it seemed impossible that he had ever been able to fit inside the tiny vehicle in the first place. He arched his back with an audible crack and gave an exaggerated sigh of relief, then turned a slow circle as if surveying the pastoral landscape.

There wasn't much to see. The Fiat was parked on the side of a narrow, poorly maintained country road, right beside a square tower-like structure—two stories high, but only about ten feet on each side. It was a transformer station, if the web of power lines sprouting from it and radiating out in every direction was any indication. A few farmhouses lay scattered here and there across the undulating hills. About a hundred yards behind them stood a tiny chapel, barely bigger than a phone booth, topped with the distinctive domed cupola common to the Eastern Orthodox church. The gray sky, which seemed to threaten rain, but couldn't quite commit to it, lent an aura of melancholy to the place, which Bones did not fail to pick up on.

"This place reminds me of where I grew up," he remarked as the car's other two occupants emerged. "And not in a good way. How far is it to Paris?"

"Paris?" asked Corey Dean. Behind a droop of thinning red-hair, his forehead wrinkled in earnest consternation. He turned a few degrees until he was facing northwest and pointed.

"It's about a thousand miles in that direction." He

shook his head. "I thought Native Americans were supposed to have an infallible sense of direction."

"I am far from the lands of my ancestors," Bones replied, his already deep voice lowering an octave, affecting grave solemnity. He caught the eye of the man who had just gotten out on the opposite side of the vehicle—his friend and business partner, Dane Maddock—and winked. "A thousand miles? That can't be right. I thought Bulgaria and France were neighbors?"

"You're thinking of Belgium," replied Corey. "They're totally different countries. Belgium is like France's version of Canada. Bulgaria is in the Balkans— "

"I thought Canada was France's version of Canada," Bones cut in.

"He's just messing with you, Corey," Maddock said. "He knows exactly where we are. We've been here before." He paused a moment, searched his memories, and then amended, "Well, not here exactly, but hereabouts."

It was entirely possible that he and Bones had passed through Bulgaria during their long stint as Navy SEALs, but if so, it had been only a stopover during transit— probably to neighboring Bosnia-Herzegovina, where they had hunted Serbian war criminals.

That seemed a lifetime ago, and a lot had happened since then.

Maddock and Bones weren't SEALs anymore. The two men had ended their military careers not long after the Balkan assignment, and had gone on to pursue their dream of being treasure hunters, specializing in marine recovery.

They were unlikely friends. Maddock was methodical, straitlaced, even, admittedly, a bit uptight. Bones was loud and obnoxious, irreverent, often politically incorrect, especially when it came to deprecating his

Cherokee heritage. They had first met during the initial phase of SEAL training, and had immediately butted heads, even coming to blows at one point. But over the years, through too many adventures to count, they had come to realize that their differences were what made them such an effective team.

Bones looked around again. "I wonder where Max is? He made it sound like this was a big production. This place should be crawling with people. I figured he'd at least have an RV."

"Maybe they cancelled the shoot on account of the weather," Corey ventured.

Bones snorted derisively. "What weather? This is nothing."

"Gotta agree with Bones," Maddock said, waving a hand through the damp air. "I don't think this could charitably be called drizzle."

Corey however stood his ground. "Shows what you know. It's not the rain that's a problem. It's the light. Or more accurately, the lack of it. When it's this dark, contrast sucks and the shots look all grainy."

It was no surprise that Corey had zeroed in on the technical detail. Maddock's treasure-hunting crew mostly comprised former military veterans, but Corey was the exception. He'd never served in the military, and fairly hated the idea of any kind of violence, save perhaps for the simulated variety found in video games. A late addition to the team, he was their resident expert on all things electronic and high-tech, which included maintenance and operation of their video equipment.

"Point to Corey," Maddock admitted.

Bones however shook his head. "Do you even watch Max's show?"

Max was Max Riddle, host of the cable television

documentary series *Maximum Mysteries*, which purported to investigate paranormal phenomena, legendary monsters and alien conspiracies—the crazier, the better. They had met Max a few months earlier in Luxor, Egypt, where he was filming a segment for his show concerning a decoration in a temple which seemed to depict what looked suspiciously like an incandescent light bulb, leading many to believe that the ancient Egyptians had possessed advanced technology, presumably given to them by aliens. Their encounter had proven fortuitous for Riddle. His cameras had been rolling when Maddock and Bones revealed their discovery of a previously unknown tomb in the Valley of the Kings, and his ratings hadn't suffered.

The invitation to join him for the filming of a new episode in Bulgaria—all expenses paid by the Bulgarian Board of Tourism—was presumably Riddle's way of saying "thank you." Upon arrival in the capital city—Sofia—they had immediately picked up the Fiat from the rental counter. The rental reservation, also courtesy of the tourism board, had clearly been made by someone unaware of Bones' size, and he hadn't exactly suffered in silence during the forty-five-minute drive into the hinterlands.

Bulgaria seemed like an odd destination for Riddle. Maddock knew almost nothing about the country, other than that it had been part of the Communist Eastern Bloc for most of his lifetime. When he thought of it at all, which was not often, he lumped it together with the other Balkan states. Even a cursory review of the Wikipedia entry for Bulgaria and its capital offered little to distinguish the eastern European nation, despite the fact that it had been continuously occupied for thousands of years, and as such, had a rich and storied history.

Maybe that was the problem. With so much history, piled up in layers, it was hard to know where to look. A Google search of "places to see in Sofia" yielded up a long list of churches and former churches repurposed into museums, a few old Roman ruins, including a public bath—evidently there were mineral hot springs running under the city—and not much else. Ordinarily, Maddock could happily lose himself in a museum, but usually he did so with some sense of purpose—a mystery that needed solving, a clue to hidden treasure that needed to be revealed.

He had no idea what he was doing in Bulgaria, aside from the fact that Max Riddle had invited them.

Maddock had seen a few episodes of Riddle's show, particularly the one where he showed off the discovery in Egypt, but he wasn't exactly a fan. Not like Bones, who ate up the crazy cryptid-UFO-conspiracy stuff like it was ice cream. Bones was not about to let Maddock refuse the invitation, especially not if it presented a chance to investigate something kooky.

Or be on TV again.

"He loves being out in nasty weather," Bones went on. "It makes him look rugged."

Maddock fought the urge to roll his eyes. The opportunity to make further comment was lost as a vehicle—a white Mercedes M-Class—appeared from around the bend to the south. The SUV slowed as it approached, pulling off the road to park behind the Fiat. Through the water-spotted windshield, Maddock could just make out the familiar grinning visage of Max Riddle in the passenger seat.

"Hellooooo," Bones said, and started forward as the doors on either side of the vehicle swung open. "Dibs."

Maddock glanced over at his friend, a little surprised

by Bones' uncharacteristic enthusiasm. "I know you've got a bro crush on Max," he muttered, "but do you have to be so obvious about it?"

"Max who?" Bones said, making a beeline for the driver's side of the vehicle. He caught hold of the door handle, holding it as if he were a doorman or valet, waiting to assist the driver. Maddock caught a flash of long blonde hair and pale skin as the person slipped from behind the wheel to disappear behind Bones' bulk.

"Oh," was all Maddock could say.

Riddle, seemingly oblivious to what was happening on the opposite side of the vehicle, advanced toward Maddock. "Dane! Glad you could make it. I guess my directions didn't lead you astray."

Maddock shook the other man's hand. "We thought maybe they had. Doesn't seem to be much happening here."

"Oh, there's a lot more going on here than meets the eye." Riddle winked. "Under the surface, so to speak."

Before Maddock could inquire further regarding the cryptic clichés, Riddle spoke again. "But where are my manners? Let me introduce you to someone." He turned and gestured toward the driver just as Bones stepped out of the way.

Maddock already knew two things about the driver—she was female, and she was gorgeous. The former assumption was based on the brief glimpse he had caught of her as she got out of the vehicle. The latter, he deduced from the intensity of Bones' reaction.

The big man was drawn to good-looking women like… Well, like a moth to a flame. Unlike the proverbial moth, Bones didn't always get burned, though he seemed incapable of sustaining a relationship longer than a few months. Those failures didn't seem to faze Bones. Or slow him down.

When Bones had zeroed in on the blonde behind the wheel, Maddock had known that she would be attractive, but when he finally got a look at her, he knew that description was inadequate. She was very pretty, but there was an aura of sweetness and sincerity about her that immediately made Maddock want to shield her from Bones' persistent overtures.

"Guys," Riddle went on, "This is Slava Kostadinova. She works for the National Board of Tourism. She made all of this possible. Slava, this is Dane Maddock, Bones Bonebrake, and…" He hesitated, looking uncertainly at Corey for a moment. "I'm sorry Dane, I don't think I've actually met your plus one."

Corey seemed a little startled at being the focus of attention. His gaze went from Riddle to Slava, his face reddening in embarrassment and timidity.

Bones laughed. "Dude. Breathe."

"This is Corey Dean," Maddock said. "Your invitation mentioned bringing along someone who's tech-savvy. Corey is the best."

Corey seemed to recover his wits. He nodded and took a step forward, but then hesitated again, as if unsure whether to approach Riddle or Slava. He decided instead to simply stay put. He gave a sheepish wave, and then cleared his throat. "I love your show." His eyes went to Riddle. "Your show, I mean." He turned to Slava. "I don't know if you have a show."

"If you do," Bones put in, "I'd watch. Is it on streaming? Maybe you and me can Netflix and chill."

Maddock braced himself. *Shots fired,* he thought.

When Bones uttered one of his horrible pick-up lines, the reaction was rarely ambiguous. Either the woman on the receiving end would reject him with extreme prejudice, or respond in kind with her own brand of flirtatious banter.

Slava did neither. Instead, she offered the most innocent smile Maddock had ever seen, and spoke. "No, I don't have a show. Not yet. But Max says he is going to make me a star."

She looked over at Max and winked. Her English was clear, but flavored with a distinctive Slavic accent. After a moment, she turned her attention to Corey of all people.

"You know that Bulgaria is the new high-tech capital of the Balkans. Sofia, our capital city, is the Silicon Valley of Eastern Europe."

Corey reddened again, but then broke into a beaming smile. "I did know that actually. I was reading about some of the tech start-ups that are breaking out here. And block-chain is really taking off here, too."

"Uh, oh," Bones muttered to Maddock. "Nerdgasm alert."

Maddock couldn't help but grin. "Jealous?"

"Who me? Nah. She's got future trophy wife written all over her."

"Never stopped you before."

Bones laughed. "Won't stop me now, either."

Maddock decided to intervene before either of his friends could embarrass themselves further. "Max, where's your crew? Or is the shoot happening somewhere else?"

Riddle nodded smoothly, like a used-car salesman. "Right. So, funny story about that."

Maddock glanced over at Bones, who met his gaze, mirroring his suspicions. The TV host was up to something.

"I'll explain everything," Riddle went on. "First, let me show you something."

Without waiting for a reply, he turned away and

headed to the rear of the SUV where he opened the cargo hatch. "Check this out. Corey… It's Corey, right? You're going to love this."

Slava flashed her signature winning smile and then headed back to join Riddle. Corey moved immediately to follow. Maddock and Bones did so as well, but with the kind of wariness they typically reserved for crossing minefields.

Corey, arriving ahead of them, let out an appreciative whistle. "Is that what I think it is?"

"If you think it's a DJI Inspire 2 with 6K RAW video and a CineCore 2.1 imaging processor… then, yeah, that's exactly what it is."

"Cool." Corey sounded like someone in the grip of a religious experience. "Can I… Touch it?"

"Touch it?" Riddle laughed. "Corey, my man, how would you like to fly it?"

Maddock rounded the corner and looked over Corey's shoulder. The focus of Corey's attention looked like a robotic spider. Maddock immediately recognized it as a quad-copter camera drone—a scaled up version of the one Corey sometimes used when conducting aerial surveys of potential dive sites. In addition to the drone, which took up nearly half of the cargo area, there were several plastic totes. One of them was stuffed with several coils of rope. Another was filled with various pieces of electronic hardware, including several GoPro cameras and battery packs.

"Geez," Bones muttered, joining the group. "I was gonna tell you two to get a room, but after looking at all this stuff, I'm afraid of what you might do."

Maddock's instincts tingled with suspicion. "I'm reminded of an old saying, 'Beware basic cable television personalities bearing gifts.'"

Riddle affected mock outrage. "Basic? You wound me, Dane."

Maddock gestured at the equipment. "GoPros. Camera drones. This isn't production equipment. What's going on here?"

"Actually, they've filmed several major motion pictures with that drone. It's state of the art."

"Cut the crap, Max. You invited us here to watch you film your show. Where's your crew?" He stopped as the answer dawned. "We're your crew."

Max raised his hands in a "slow down" gesture. "Let me explain."

Maddock exchanged a glance with Bones. To Maddock's dismay, the big man looked unperturbed by Riddle's conspicuous failure to refute the charge.

Riddle took a breath, then blew it out. "Okay, so you remember Egypt? That show was pure magic, and it was all because of you guys. The raw video you shot with that remote of yours? It was compelling."

"We weren't in Egypt for your show, Max. The fact that we ran into you was just a coincidence." *One I'm beginning to regret*, Maddock thought, but didn't say aloud.

"Oh, I get that. But I mean, that's the whole point. I mean, we do phone video and camera stuff trying to get that look, but it still feels produced. Know what I mean?" He didn't wait for an answer. "So then I got this crazy idea. What if, instead of trying to get my producers to recreate what you guys did, how about I just let you guys do what you do?"

"So you want us in your show," Bones said. He shrugged. "I'm in. We should probably keep Maddock behind the camera, though. Dude's got a great face for radio, if you know what I mean."

"We're not going to be on either side of the camera," Maddock said, emphatically. "This isn't what we do, Max. We aren't TV personalities, and we aren't professional filmmakers."

"But don't you see? That's the hook. You aren't *personalities.* You're the real deal."

Before Maddock could protest again, Bones leaned close. "Dude, let's hear him out. This could be fun."

"Seconded," Corey put in, his gaze still fixed on the quad-copter drone.

Maddock knew his friends were firmly under Riddle's spell, but he couldn't shake the feeling that the man wasn't being entirely honest with them. "If we do this…" He shook his head. "What's in it for us? And don't say 'exposure.' Exposure doesn't pay the bills."

"You'll get a percentage."

"A percentage?" Maddock's Spidey-sense tingled again. "No offense, Max, but maybe we should be talking to someone at the network."

Riddle pursed his lips together. "We aren't really at the network stage with this."

"Not at the network stage?" The tingle was now a persistent alarm. "What does that mean? Is this for your show, or isn't it?"

Riddle equivocated. "There isn't really a show right now."

"Dude, what are you talking about?" Bones said. "They do a fricking marathon every weekend."

"Right. The old seasons will continue to run for a couple more years. But we're going to shop this idea around. What we're doing here is mostly a proof of concept, though I'm hoping we'll get enough to cut it into a pilot."

Bones stiffened and put his fists on his hips in a

defiant pose. "Are you saying Maximum Mysteries got the axe? How is that possible? You told us the Egypt show was ratings gold."

Riddle grimaced. "It was. Unfortunately, it kind of raised the bar. The network wanted more of that, but they weren't willing to give me the budget to make it happen."

"Did you quit, or did they fire you?" Maddock asked.

Riddle shrugged. "I think of it as a conscious uncoupling."

"And now you're trying to launch a new show, only instead of a small budget, you've got zilch. And you figured we'd work cheap."

Slava chose this moment to speak up. "Mr. Maddock, the Board of Tourism is sponsoring this expedition. We are very excited that Mr. Riddle has chosen to launch his new series here in Bulgaria." She flashed her dazzling smile again. "I know this wasn't what you were expecting, but please, won't you give him a chance? The Board is covering all your expenses while you are here. What have you got to lose?"

Maddock could think of several things—foremost of which were his time and sanity—but Slava's smile disarmed him.

"It sucks that they cancelled the show," Bones muttered, sounding truly dejected. He glanced over at Maddock, then back to Riddle. "You think we can help get you back on the air?"

"We're looking at all our options."

Maddock didn't want to know what that might mean. He shook his head. "All right, Max. Fine. We're here. What exactly is your plan?"

Riddle let out an audible sigh of relief, nodded gratefully in Slava's direction, and then clapped his hands together. "You know what, we should be getting this on video. I'll have to explain it all anyway." He turned to Corey. "It's probably too wet to fly the drone out here, but we can use it as a handheld. You know how to do that?"

Corey had already picked up the device and started pushing buttons. After a few seconds, he flashed a thumbs-up and pointed the drone's camera at Riddle.

"Great. Just point the camera at me. The computer will keep me in focus?"

"Do I need to say 'action' or anything?"

"If you'd like."

"Then… Action!"

2

Riddle seemed to undergo a physical transformation. His expression became serious, his carriage more erect, and when he spoke, looking directly at the camera, his voice was low and full of gravitas. "We are in western Bulgaria, in the village of Tsarichina, not far from the capital Sofia, to investigate one of the strangest mysteries you've never heard of. This is the story of the Tsarichina Hole."

Maddock glanced at Bones, curious to see if his friend recognized the name. Bones shook his head, indicating he did not.

Riddle allowed a few seconds to pass, probably to give some wiggle room for the editing process, and then resumed, clearly channeling a well-rehearsed mental script. "The story begins almost thirty years ago. It is December, 1990. Bulgaria has just thrown off the oppressive yoke of Communist rule and is looking to join the modern world. It is a time of great uncertainty. There is economic and social unrest. And then, in the midst of it all, the Bulgarian army arrives at this place, in the little village of Tsarichina, and begins a massive excavation. They started right there." He gestured toward the open ground east of the transformer building.

"They called it 'Operation: Sun Ray.' Over the next two years, Bulgarian army diggers would remove tons of earth—with heavy digging equipment, as well as pick and shovel. The estimated cost of the project was reportedly over nine million dollars. Then, in November of 1992, after clearing a tunnel over 180 meters long, the government shut down the excavation, and ordered the entrance to Tsarichina Hole filled up with concrete, and buried."

"Government cover-up," Bones whispered. "Typical."

Maddock scanned the open area again. The ground was flat and unremarkable, with some scruffy vegetation and a single tree that looked to be about the right size to have been planted three decades earlier. There was nothing at all to indicate an undertaking like what Riddle had just described.

"It's unclear what the government was looking for here, but rumors abound. Many believe they were searching for the lost golden treasure of Bulgaria's greatest leader, Tsar Samuil, who ruled in the Tenth Century. But if that's true, what prompted them to look in Tsarichina? And why did they abruptly end the search and seal off the excavation?

"All official documents relating to Operation: Sun Ray have been sealed—and possibly destroyed—by the government, but in his book on the Tsarichina Phenomenon, Colonel Tzvetko Stefanov—who led the excavation—reveals that they were taking their directions from a pair of psychic remote viewers—Rumen Nikolov and Maria Ionova."

Despite wanting to roll his eyes at the mention of psychics, Maddock had to admit that Riddle had uncovered quite a story. If nothing else, the prospect of buried treasure had just made the trip a little more interesting.

"Rumen and Maria weren't helping the Bulgarian government look for the gold of Samuil however," Riddle went on. "They were dialed into something far more mysterious. They claimed to have been receiving messages that would lead them to an underground chamber where they would find an entity they called 'the first human ancestor.'

"Six meters down, the excavation uncovered a rectangular stone that Stefanov designated Object Number One. The stone was adorned with strange symbols in a language no one could read. No one but Rumen and Maria. The psychics revealed that the slab was a kind of bio-hazard warning, and warned that moving it would unleash an apocalyptic plague.

"Stefanov took the advice seriously and ordered the soldiers to begin a new excavation to work around the hazard. They soon uncovered a tunnel with a smooth ceiling, leading to a spiral passage that descended over 160 meters where they encountered another strange barrier—a metal slab in the shape of a concave lens. Carved into the wall beside the door was the likeness of a gigantic humanoid figure, which Rumen confirmed to be the ancient human ancestor.

"The soldiers removed the metal slab to reveal a tunnel with a silvery-gray floor, and walls covered with more of the same strange language. But when Stefanov and the other soldiers tried to enter the tunnel, a powerful, invisible force knocked them back.

"Stefanov was determined to continue and began plans to excavate around the impenetrable barrier, but someone in the Bulgarian government decided to consult famed mystic Baba Vanga. Baba Vanga confirmed that they were close to the remains of the ancient ancestor—who was neither male nor female—and further warned that they should leave it alone.

"At first, Stefanov didn't take the warning seriously, but then tragedy struck. Maria Ionova, one of the psychic remote viewers, died unexpectedly. Shortly thereafter, Colonel Stefanov gave the order to seal the site permanently.

"But that's not the end of this strange story."

Riddle paused again, and then began walking toward the transformer building. When he reached the door, he turned to face the camera again.

"During the excavation, witnesses recorded fifteen separate UFO sightings. Six months after the dig ended, Rumen returned to Tsarichina, accompanied by a team of scientists, to investigate the UFO sightings. Over the next two weeks, they logged twenty-one encounters, along with other strange phenomena, including poltergeists, and an unexplained fire that nearly destroyed the camp. The scientists believed they were dealing with an extraterrestrial life form, hostile to humanity.

"Then, one night near the end of July, an unidentified object landed behind the hill—" Riddle paused and looked past Corey and the camera drone. "Right over there. Rumen went to investigate. When he returned, he reported having met with strange humanoid beings—the same species as the First Human Ancestor buried under Tsarichina. They told him that the entity he had been communicating with was indeed the first intelligent life form to walk the earth, and was neither alive nor dead, but rather existed in a state outside time. They revealed that the original excavation had come within six meters of the resting place of the entity.

"They also gave him a clear message: Do not disturb."

Riddle fell silent again, as if to allow his future viewers time to digest the account of the strange encounter. Corey sidestepped away in order to get a different angle.

"To this day," Riddle continued, "Tsarichina remains a hotbed of UFO activity, even earning the nickname, 'Bulgaria's Area 51.' Locals and visitors often report strange blue lights moving about near the ground. For thirty years, the Bulgarian government has refused to comment on Operation: Sun Ray, refused to even acknowledge that any of it happened."

He allowed another dramatic pause, but this time, only for a few seconds. "But now, there's been an exciting development. Officially, the Tsarichina Hole was sealed under several hundred cubic yards of concrete." He half-turned, one hand coming to rest on the door of the building. "But what nobody realized, or even suspected, was that Colonel Stefanov left a back door into the excavation."

As much as he wanted to dismiss it all as a lot of woo-woo nonsense, Maddock realized he had forgotten to breathe. Part of him thought the whole thing was an elaborate urban myth, but the other part of him was hanging on Riddle's every word.

Riddle stayed like that for several seconds—a dramatic pause—and then turned to face the door. His right hand went to the deadbolt lock, and now Maddock saw that he was holding a key, which he slotted into place and turned. Riddle then reached for the doorknob, gave it a twist and pulled.

Maddock almost started as the door swung open. Aside from the creak of long unused hinges, nothing unusual happened. Beyond the doorframe, the interior was mostly taken up by the large boxy electrical transformer, which sat on the concrete floor, emitting a low hum.

Riddle took a step inside and pointed down at a rusty metal drain cover, about two feet across, mounted flush with the concrete slab. "Under this drain cover is a short tunnel that connects with the entrance to the original excavation. The Bulgarian government has given us exclusive access to the site. Now, we're going to take you to a place where no one has gone for nearly thirty years, to discover the truth about a mysterious object that might spell doom for humanity, and just maybe find the last resting place of the extraterrestrial entity known as the First Human Ancestor. Join me as we go inside the Tsarichina Hole."

Riddle's voice rose as he neared the climax of his little speech, but once the last line was delivered, he fell silent, staring at the camera with an unreal intensity. He held the pose for what must have been a full thirty seconds, and then gave a slight nod.

"And cut," he said, and then turned to Maddock and Bones. "So what do you think, guys. Are you in?"

Bones didn't give Maddock a chance to say no. "Hells yeah!"

3

Rather than dive right into the tunnel, Riddle spent some more time outside the transformer building, "shooting B-roll," with Corey working the camera drone and Slava providing an audience. Maddock and Bones spent the time inventorying the equipment Riddle had brought along. In addition to the rope, there were climbing harnesses, helmets, gloves, and rappelling devices—enough gear for all of them.

"I guess now we know why he invited us along," Maddock remarked to Bones. "He wants us to do all the heavy lifting."

Bones gave him a sidelong glance. "So? It's kind of what we do."

Maddock gave a noncommittal grunt. "Would have been nice if he'd just been up front with us. We could have brought our own gear."

"Admit it. If you had known what he had planned, you'd have found an excuse to stay home."

"Probably. I mean... Come on... Remote viewers? Aliens? Baba Vanga? Admit it, this is nutty, even by your standards."

Bones shrugged. "I'm not saying I take it at face value, but we both know that sometimes when you get past the nutty outer layer, you find an even nuttier truth."

"Fair enough."

"Besides," Bones went on. "Hanging out with that Slava chick doesn't suck."

"I don't know," Maddock retorted. "She seems a little... Hallmark Channel for you."

"Nice girls need love, too."

Maddock just shook his head.

When Riddle determined that he had gathered enough B-roll, he and Corey began the process of syncing the drone and several GoPro cameras to half-a-dozen tablet computers, which were in turn connected to a portable power supply that resembled a medium-sized beer cooler. Everyone, including Slava, was outfitted with a GoPro attached to a chest mount, and then they headed back inside the transformer building.

Riddle brought out a three foot-long metal rod with a handle at one end and a sharp hook at the other. He inserted the hook end into a small notch on the outer circumference of the drain cover, and with surprisingly little effort, lifted the cover out of the recessed opening. As he slid it aside, the sound of the metal scraping across the concrete filled the little enclosure, reverberating with bone-shaking intensity, eliciting a grimace from Maddock. When the noise stopped, they all crowded around the opening and looked down.

The uncovering revealed an unremarkable concrete pipe that descended vertically for a good fifteen feet, beyond which, there was only murky darkness.

"Yep, that's a hole," Bones said, and then looked over at Maddock. "Looks pretty intense. You better go first for once."

Maddock rolled his eyes, and then turned and headed back to the SUV to grab the climbing gear.

While Bones rigged a single line, anchored to the base of the transformer, Maddock donned one of the seat-harnesses, along with a helmet, a headlamp, and a pair of leather gloves. He then threaded a figure-8 rappelling brake onto the line and clipped it to the front of his harness with a locking carabiner. Thus equipped, and without ceremony, he sat down on the edge of the opening, and lowered himself in.

On a cliff wall, Maddock would have simply bounded down in two or three dynamic leaps, but the close confines forced him to take it slow, letting the rope dribble through his gloved fingers. Even so, the figure-8 device quickly grew warm from the friction of the rope sliding through.

Once he descended below the open end of the pipe, Maddock saw that there wasn't much further to go. The vertical shaft intersected a much larger horizontal concrete culvert, measuring at least twelve feet in diameter, the bottom six inches of which were under water.

"Hope you brought some galoshes," Maddock shouted up to the others. His voice bounced back and forth in an interference pattern of overlapping echoes, and the reply, when it came was incomprehensible. He shrugged and lowered himself down, straddling the rivulet to keep his feet dry a little longer. He payed out a couple more arm lengths of rope, then unclipped from the figure-8.

"Off rope!" he shouted. The short utterance sounded a little more coherent, as did Bones' response. A moment later, the rope was pulled back up, along with the braking device.

He knew it would take a few minutes for Bones to rig up whoever was coming next, so he decided to use the time to conduct a cursory inspection of the tunnel. There was no immediate evidence that it was anything more than what it appeared to be—a drain designed to keep heavy rains from flooding the village's power supply. Since the floor of the shed was dry, it stood to reason that the water was probably seepage, filtering down through the strata to accumulate at the bottom of the culvert. The large bore pipe ran more or less east-west, with what felt like a slight tilt down to the east, which according to Riddle was where the excavation had taken place. That meant the seepage was flowing, albeit very slowly, into the excavation, so there was a very good chance the whole thing would be underwater.

He turned his head in that direction, but the beam of his headlamp disappeared into the endless darkness.

Riddle's shout echoed down to him. "On rappel!"

Maddock turned back and took hold of the dangling rope. "On belay!"

For the next few minutes, his only job was to watch Riddle make his descent. If the TV host made a mistake or lost control, it would be Maddock's responsibility to pull hard on the rope in order to lock down the rappelling device and arrest the other man's fall. Riddle however needed no such assistance. He slid down the rope with practiced ease.

"This is amazing," he said in a low, awed voice, which Maddock realized was solely for the benefit of a future television audience. "We're inside a tunnel that leads into the controversial Bulgarian army excavation. No one has been here in over thirty years. Who knows what we'll find at the bottom?"

"Probably a lot of water," Maddock remarked. Riddle threw him a sour look, which Maddock ignored. "You should unclip."

"Oh, right." Riddle quickly unhooked and shouted up that he was off the rope. Then he sidled past Maddock and ventured a ways down the passage, supplying a running monologue as he went. Maddock tuned him out and focused his attention on belaying for the next person, who turned out to be Slava.

The Bulgarian woman was more tentative about her descent than Riddle, pausing several times in the first few feet, as if trying to find her nerve. The hesitations became less frequent, but she remained tense throughout, the rope inching out with almost painful slowness.

Maddock placed a reassuring hand on her arm, steadying her as she fumbled to unclip from the figure-8. "First time sliding down a rope?" he asked.

His intent was merely to use idle conversation to calm her down, but as soon as the words left his mouth, he realized that it sounded like something Bones might say. Fortunately, Slava took the question as intended—literally. "Yes," she said, her voice quavering a little. "I usually leave the extreme sports to the boys."

The reply struck Maddock as odd. He was so accustomed to being around capable women who enjoyed competitive sports and outdoor pursuits, that he genuinely had no idea how to interact with someone who did not. "You could have stayed up top," he managed to say.

Curiously, she nodded her head, but then said, "I must accompany Max into Tsarichina Hole to verify whatever he finds. Or does not find."

"Oh, right. That makes sense."

Just then, Bones shouted, "On rappel."

"On belay," Maddock answered, automatically.

The big man came down fast—maybe too fast—and splashed down onto the curved floor of the culvert.

"Ugh," Bones said, looking down in dismay at the water which completely covered his boots. Maddock saw that he had four coils of rope slung across his broad chest like bandoliers.

"Where's Corey?" Maddock asked.

"He decided to stay topside and run things from there."

Maddock wasn't surprised by this, but Riddle must have overheard because he hastened back down to join them. "He won't be much use up there. The WiFi signal only has a range of about twenty-five feet or so, and it's line of sight."

Bones shrugged. "He said something about that. And he also said he could figure out a way to turn our phones into signal repeaters. Honestly, I sort of stopped paying attention, but it sounded like he knew what he was talking about."

Riddle frowned but then nodded. "I guess that's fine. Worst case scenario, we'll just store the raw footage on the devices and then upload it once we get back up. I just hope we don't run out of memory before we reach the bottom. You only get one chance to record a first look."

Maddock looked over at him. "You really think we're going to find something down here?"

Riddle shrugged. "In my world, even finding nothing is something."

"Tell that to Geraldo Rivera," Bones remarked. "He's still trying to live down Al Capone's vault."

"Actually, that moment made him a household name," Riddle countered. "There's no such thing as bad publicity. But this is different. He did that on live TV. We'll know the truth, one way or the other, before this goes out into the world. We'll control the narrative. If there's nothing there, we'll focus on how the Bulgarian government was hoodwinked into throwing away millions of dollars and thousands of man hours digging this hole. And if there's something there…" He grinned, leaving the rest to the imagination.

They started down the culvert, doing their best to straddle the water and stay dry. Maddock expected that they would soon discover that the excavation was fully submerged, thus denying Riddle the definitive proof he sought, but kept this pessimistic supposition to himself.

He was glad he did, for just a little ways further down, the culvert ended, opening into a much larger square cut passage that sloped downward at about a twenty percent grade. The back wall, where the culvert emerged, was relatively smooth gray concrete, but the passage beyond was rough cut sedimentary rock. Maddock could see the grooved scars left by heavy duty drilling and digging equipment. The water streaming from the end of the culvert flowed out into a thin, irregular layer across the floor where it either evaporated or soaked into the stone, leaving the passage mostly dry.

"We are now standing at the entrance of the Tsarichina Hole excavation," Riddle said. "Officially, the hole was filled in with concrete, but now we know that only a small portion of it was actually filled to plug the entrance."

"Makes sense," Maddock mused aloud. "If this hole really is as deep as you said, then it would have taken a massive amount of concrete to fill it."

Riddle nodded. "Which would have added a lot more expense to a project that had already consumed millions."

"If they left a back door," Bones mused, "then it probably means they intended to come back and keep working in secret."

"That may have been their intent," Slava said, breaking her long silence. "But there is no evidence that anyone ever did. It would be very hard to keep a secret like that. People have been paying attention to Tsarichina."

"So why didn't they come back?" Bones pressed.

"Here is what I think. Colonel Stefanov believed he would be able to get permission to continue the work in secret, but the government did not agree. Many scientific experts testified that there was nothing special about the excavation, and even accused Rumen of being a fraud.

Stefanov lost the support of the government. Nobody else wanted to reopen the excavation, either because they were afraid of what they might find, or because they feared they would find proof that it had been a sham, which would destroy the careers of any who supported it in the first place."

Maddock nodded, impressed by her insights. "So why is your government allowing us to investigate it? Thirty years isn't that long. Some of those people are probably still in positions of power. Aren't they worried that we might embarrass them if all we find is a dry hole?"

Slava flashed her winning smile. "It is as Max says. There's no such thing as bad publicity. No matter what we find down here, it will bring visitors to Bulgaria, and that is good for everyone."

"And on that note," Riddle said, "let's stop speculating and find out what's really down there."

The passage continued straight for about fifty feet and then made a sharp turn to the right. A few yards later, there was another turn, this time to the left, and then another left turn just past that. A few more yards brought them another right turn after which the slope of the passage increased several degrees.

Riddle stopped suddenly and turned to face them all. "Do you realize what that was?"

Rather than offer an explanation, he backtracked to the first turn and then began counting off steps. "Okay, this first section is about ten feet long. Then we've got a section that's about six feet, and then another ten which puts us more or less on the same trajectory we were on before the first turn, but with six feet of solid rock between there and here.

"Stefanov said that they found Object Number One at six meters down. Rumen Nikolov warned them not to break the seal, so they dug this passage to go around it." He pointed to the wall behind them. "Object Number One is right there."

"Wasn't there supposed to be a stone tablet of some kind?" Maddock countered.

Riddle frowned at this apparent contradiction, but then brightened a little. "It's possible that he never actually laid eyes on the tablet. He was taking his cues from Rumen, who might have seen the object psychically."

"That's convenient."

"Dude," Bones said. "Keep an open mind. You of all people know how weird this world really is."

"If Rumen was telling the truth," Riddle said, clearly speaking for the cameras, "then behind this wall, there's a pathogen capable of wiping out all life on earth. I don't know about you, but that's not something I want to mess with. Let's keep moving."

There was another right turn about ten feet further along. The passage continued for another fifty feet or more, but Maddock noticed it wasn't quite as straight as the first section. And that wasn't the only difference. "It's getting kind of close in here."

Maddock was not normally claustrophobic, and had explored more caves than he could count, but for some reason, the passage felt especially confining. He could almost feel the physical weight of so much earth suspended above him.

"When they started the excavation," Riddle explained. "they expected to find what they were looking for in a matter of days. As they went deeper, they began having problems. The rock was harder than they anticipated. Their digging equipment kept mysteriously breaking down."

"You mentioned UFO sightings," Bones interjected.

"Unexplained mechanical and electrical failures often accompany a close encounter."

Riddle gave him a knowing look, then went on. "They had to finish the excavation the hard way—pick and shovel. By that point, their only concern was in making the passage big enough to accommodate one person at a time."

Maddock glanced over at Slava, curious to see how she was holding up, given her stated dislike for "extreme sports." She noticed his attention and managed a wan smile.

The passage continued through a series of random turns for several hundred more feet. The slope remained mostly the same, though there were a few places where the way became so steep that Maddock almost suggested using the rope as a safety measure, and probably would have done so if not for the fact that the passage had shrunk to the point where they could brace themselves against the walls as they traversed those sections.

"I think we're in the spiral passage Stefanov described," Riddle announced. "But it's not what I was expecting."

"How so?" inquired Bones.

"He made it sound almost like something they discovered. An existing tunnel. There are sketches that show Roman-style barrel vault construction. But this doesn't look any different than the rest of the excavation."

Maddock shone his light on the walls, confirming Riddle's observation. Everything had the same rough-hewn look they'd seen from the beginning. Then he noticed something else. There were dark, glistening spots of moisture oozing from the rock.

So much for a dry hole, he thought.

As they continued down the irregular spiral, the

dampness increased to the point that water dripped from the ceiling and walls, forming rivulets that streamed down the passage ahead of them. Maddock felt sure they would round a corner and find themselves facing an impassable pool.

He was partly right.

Only a few minutes later, they reached a section of the passage that was completely underwater. The constant slope meant that the water was very shallow at first, but would become increasingly deep with each step forward until there was nowhere left to go.

Riddle stood at the edge of the water, shining his light ahead. There was another bend, indicating that the excavation had continued, but if they were going to keep exploring it would mean getting wet.

"End of the line," Maddock said. "Maybe this was the 'invisible force' that turned them back. Not an alien force field, but water."

"I want to see what's at the end," Riddle insisted. "We're close. I'm sure of it. How would you guys feel about coming back here with dive gear. Or we could have that little ROV of yours sent over by Fed Ex."

Maddock groaned a little at the suggestion, though he'd been expecting it. Riddle knew of their experience working in submerged environments. "I don't know Max. Shipping Uma could get pretty expensive." Uma was the nickname Bones had given to their remotely-operated-vehicle, a sort of underwater camera drone that they had used in several treasure hunts, including the operation in Egypt.

Slava shook her head, but then said something that seemed to contradict the gesture. "My government will pay for whatever you need, Mr. Maddock. We want to see what's down there, too."

Maddock wondered why, if that was true, the Bulgarians hadn't simply re-opened the excavation themselves. Before he could ask however, Bones spoke up. "Maybe we don't need to wait. You said we're almost to the end and my feet are already wet. Since we're here, we might as well go as far as we can."

Without waiting for an answer, he pushed past Riddle and stepped into the water. His first step barely made a splash. His second rose up halfway to his ankle. The next stride forward completely immersed his foot, and with each successive step, a little more of him disappeared under the surface. By the time he reached the bend, the water was halfway up his thighs. He stopped there, shining his light ahead.

"Well, the good news is, it's not freezing," he called back to the others.

"And the bad news?" Maddock asked.

"Why does there have to be bad news?"

"Because we're just lucky like that."

Bones chuckled. "Well, I'm not sure if this is bad news or good. But I don't think we're going to need Uma after all."

"Why not?" Riddle asked.

"Come and see."

Riddle immediately ventured forward, splashing down the tunnel. He pushed past Bones and disappeared from view, but Maddock could still hear his voice. "I don't get it. This isn't how Stefanov described it at all."

Before Maddock knew what was happening, Slava stepped forward into the water, hastening to see for herself.

"So much for leaving it to the boys," he muttered, and then waded in after her.

Bones had not been lying about the water

temperature. He felt an initial chill as it soaked into his boots, and saturated the fabric of his jeans, but once he was wet, the sensation of being cold passed quickly. He forgot about it completely when he rounded the corner and saw what the others were looking at.

Five feet past the bend, the passage simply ended.

Riddle had gone all the way forward, into waist deep water, to examine the rough wall where the Bulgarian army excavation had terminated. "This isn't right," he said, shaking his head. "There's supposed to be a door. And a stone figure depicting the First Human Ancestor."

"There was supposed to be a ton of bootleg hooch in Al Capone's vault, too," Bones remarked, though Maddock could hear real disappointment in the big man's tone.

"So. It was all a lie," Slava said.

Her tone was flat, matter of fact, but there was an undercurrent of satisfaction in her voice, as if this was exactly what she had expected. She waded forward to stand beside Riddle, and reached out for the wall, as if physical contact was necessary to provide absolute confirmation.

But as she placed her hands against the wall, there was a noise like a tree limb snapping, and then both Riddle and Slava vanished.

4

Before he could utter a cry of alarm, Maddock was swept off his feet. In an instant, the still pool in which he stood had transformed into a rushing, irresistible torrent, and he was caught in it. The raging water engulfed him completely, pulling at him, trying to carry him along like a piece of driftwood, but something kept him from moving... No, not something, but someone.

Bones had one hand clamped on his right shoulder, and the other gripping the wall of the passage to prevent himself from being swept away.

After only a second or two, the fury of the current seemed to abate. Maddock was no longer fully immersed in it, but merely laying in what felt like a shallow wave retreating from a beach. In the time it took for him to rise up on his elbows, the water had completely drained away, vanished into the gaping hole in the floor where Slava and Riddle had been standing only a moment before.

"Max! Slava!" Maddock called out as he started for the newly created opening. He only managed a single step before Bones hauled him back.

"Hold on," Bones said, his tone urgent. "Take it slow."

Maddock immediately grasped the reason for Bones' warning. The excavation had ended above a hollow space, possibly a limestone karst formation, and three decades of water seeping through the rock and accumulating down at the lowest point had been steadily dissolving the floor of the passage. The added weight of Max and Slava had been just enough to cause the floor to crumble into a sinkhole, and there was a very good chance that additional weight might hasten further collapse.

Maddock nodded to indicate that he understood, but wasn't about to give up on the others. "Hold my legs," he said, and rolled over onto his belly, facing the hole.

"I've got a better idea," Bones said. He unlimbered one of the coils of rope, tied a quick bowline knot in one end, and then handed the resulting loop to Maddock. "Clip in."

Maddock took the rope and hooked it to the loop on the front of his climbing harness. Bones payed out more rope, which he looped around his upper torso, and then sat back on the floor of the passage with his legs spread out, the soles of his boots jammed against the sides of the passage.

"All right," Bones said, "Now you can go."

"Moving," Maddock said, and then began sliding toward the edge of the sinkhole again, shouting as he moved. "Max!"

To his astonishment and relief, he heard Riddle's answering cry. "Dane!"

"Are you okay? Is Slava with you?" He reached out for the edge of the fissure, hooked his fingers over the lip, and began cautiously pulling himself toward it.

"We're both okay," Riddle replied. "Just a little wet."

Maddock inched forward until he was able to peer down into the hole. The beam of his headlight was reflected back from the rippling surface of a body of water, some thirty feet or so below. It took him a moment to spot Riddle and Slava—they were no longer directly below, but had found dry ground—a little rock shelf that jutted out into the water, about twenty feet or so from where they had fallen in. Both were conscious and looked shaken and bedraggled, but otherwise uninjured.

"I'm going to drop a rope down to you." He rolled onto his side to look back at Bones. "Looks like we'll need about sixty feet."

Bones let out a little more slack on Maddock's safety line, and then shucked off a second coil of rope. "Not going to be easy to pull them out," he said as he readied the rope for use. "No good anchors here."

"We'll have to make do," Maddock replied. "Between the two of us, we should be able to—"

With another loud crack, the stone beneath Maddock collapsed, plunging him into the sinkhole. He flailed his arms reflexively, seeking out the safety line even as it went taut, snapping him around into an out of control windmill.

He heard Bones shout a warning, and then dropped another foot before jolting to a halt. A faint scrabbling sound reached him, followed by a shower of rock fragments. Despite his best efforts to brace himself against the sides of the passage, Bones was being pulled toward the edge.

Another abrupt drop, another violent jolt.

Maddock knew that Bones didn't have a prayer of finding a stable position to arrest his fall, much less begin pulling him back.

"Slack!" he shouted. "Slack. Let it out."

Maddock didn't know if Bones would be able to comply in the moment or two left to them, so he did the only thing he could. He pulled on the line, lifting himself just enough to lighten the load against his harness, and then with his free hand, unclipped the carabiner. As soon as the rope loop was free of the shackle, he let go.

As he fell, Maddock twisted, trying to reposition himself so that he would splash down more or less on his backside. It wasn't a high fall, and the fact that Riddle and

Slava hadn't sustained any injuries in their completely uncontrolled fall led him to believe that the water below was fairly deep, but he wasn't going to risk a broken leg by going in feet first.

It was the right call. He plunged into the water, and then, as he was completely engulfed, felt his butt scrape against solid rock. Cushioned by the layer of water, the impact wasn't enough to cause injury, but as he rebounded back to the surface, he realized he had a new concern. The water wasn't as still as it had appeared from above. There was a current—not a fast one, but nevertheless constant— pulling him away from where he'd gone in, pulling him toward the outcropping where Riddle and Slava had washed up.

He rolled over, fumbling to plant his boot soles on the bed of the underground river, which he judged to be only about four or five feet deep.

It turned out to be closer to five. His natural buoyancy kept him just high enough in the water that he could not get a purchase, and so was dragged along by the current.

Abandoning the effort to stand, he leaned forward and reached out with both arms, pulling himself through the water with long overhand swim strokes, kicking his feet hard to propel him closer to the edge of the flow. The current quickened, creating eddies that threatened to swirl him back out into the middle of the channel, so he dropped his feet again, and this time, felt his toes dragging along in water that was only about two feet deep.

A light flashed in his face—someone's headlamp shining right at him, and only a few feet away. He dug in and then thrust himself toward it, reaching out with both hands hoping to snare the outcropping. Instead, he felt hands close around his wrists, and then he was being pulled out of the water, up onto the relatively dry ground.

He was vaguely aware of voices—Riddle and Slava—asking if he was all right, but for a few seconds, all he could do was lie there, taking deep breaths until the adrenaline finally drained out of his bloodstream. When the jitters finally stopped, he pushed himself up to a sitting position.

He took a moment to take in their new surroundings. The walls were a pale color, unnaturally smooth in some places, particularly near the water line. High above the flowing water, the roof was studded with stalactites that looked like dripping candle wax. Unlike the passage above, this was a natural cavern, carved out by the flow of the underground river rather than tools and human labor.

"You okay, Dane?" Riddle asked again.

"I'm okay, Just bruised my dignity."

Riddle clapped his shoulder. "I know the feeling."

Maddock looked up at him sidelong to avoid shining his headlamp directly into the man's eyes. "You sound pretty upbeat for someone who's stranded in a sinkhole."

"I'd say so."

Maddock raised an eyebrow. He looked past Riddle to Slava. Judging by her pinched expression, she did not share Riddle's *joie de vivre.*

"Don't you get it?" Riddle went on. "Nikolov told Colonel Stefanov that the excavation got within six meters of the resting place of the First Human Ancestor."

He pointed up at the dark hole in the ceiling through which they had entered. "Looks like about six meters to me."

"I'd say closer to ten," Maddock replied.

"That's not the point, Dane. The remote viewers sensed that they were close to something, and they were. If they'd have kept going, they would have found this."

"Found what, Max? An underground river? That's all this is."

"That's all we've seen so far. We need to have a look around."

Maddock shook his head. "What we need to do is get out of this hole." He cupped a hand to his mouth and shouted, "Bones! Can you hear me?"

"Loud and clear," came the reply. "But I don't think I'm going to be able to pull you out of there. Not without a better anchor."

"Better head back up. Tell Corey he's going to have to suck it up and help out down here."

"Will do."

Riddle chose that moment to shout, practically in Maddock's ear. "Tell him to bring the drone. We can use it to scope out this cavern."

Maddock rolled his eyes, but Bones just shouted another affirmative. "Sit tight," he finished, "I'll be right back."

"You heard the man," Maddock said, sinking down onto his haunches. "It'll probably take him an hour to make the round trip, so we might as well relax. I don't suppose anyone brought along a granola bar?"

"What if they can't pull us up?" Slava asked, sounding more than a little worried.

"Bones will figure something out," Maddock replied confidently. "Worst case scenario, he has to call in a rescue team."

Rather than easing her concerns, this suggestion only seemed to heighten Slava's anxiety.

"Maybe there's another way out," suggested Riddle. "This river has to empty somewhere."

"Somewhere may be an aquifer that's even deeper than we are right now. Even if it does come out somewhere we want to be, there's too much risk. The river might flow through cracks that are too small for us to fit through. Or through sections that are completely submerged. How long can you hold your breath, Max?"

Slava shook her head. "He's right. It is like Dyavolsko Garlo—Devil's Throat Cave—in the south near the Rhodope Mountains. It is the second largest cave in Bulgaria. A river flows into it from a waterfall, almost forty meters high, and then drains away through a submerged passage. It eventually joins with an underground river only one hundred fifty meters away, but nothing that falls into Devil's Throat ever comes out the other side. Scientists have used dye to show that it takes water more than ninety minutes to come out."

"I've heard about Devil's Throat," Riddle said. "A lot of scholars believe it was the passage that took Orpheus into the Underworld. It's also rumored to be the Abyss described in the Bible, where the fallen angels who sired the Nephilim were imprisoned." He grinned. "It's actually the next place I want to explore for the show."

Slava frowned. "In 1970s, two SCUBA divers disappeared trying to explore the hidden channel. Their bodies were never found."

Maddock gave her a nod of acknowledgement. "Exactly my point. We're not going to take chances like that. Not when Bones and Corey are right up there, ready to pull us back out."

Riddle crossed his arms over his chest and frowned. "Well can we at least look around a little while we're here?"

Maddock recalled how the current had almost carried him away, or at least it had seemed that way. He had been disoriented after the fall, and had probably panicked just a little.

"The current isn't very powerful," he told them, "but if you lose your footing and fall in, it might be strong enough to take you somewhere you don't want to go."

"I'll be careful."

Maddock sighed. "Our best chance of doing this will be to stay together, arms locked together. I'm talking deathgrip tight. If one of us slips, the other two have to keep him… or her… from going in." He turned to Slava. "If you don't want to do this…"

"I will try," she said, sounding none-too-enthusiastic. "If there is something here, I want to see with my own eyes."

"Solid," Max said, a little too eagerly.

"All right," Maddock said. "We'll go upstream. That way, if we fall and get caught in the current, we'll be able to come right back here."

He slid from the ledge and lowered himself into the river. The stone riverbed under his feet was smooth and slippery. He felt the current immediately, not quite powerful enough to knock him down, but not something to be taken for granted. Keeping a wide stance for balance, he reached out a hand to the others. "Slava, you're next."

She swallowed nervously, but took his hand, and then tentatively stepped into the water. For a second or two, she jerked his arm back and forth, overcorrecting in her attempts to keep her balance, but he kept a firm grip on her and she did not fall. When she was finally steady, he guided her away from the ledge and hooked his left arm around her right elbow. Then, he reached back to Riddle. "Your turn, Max."

Riddle's transition went smoothly, and a few seconds later, the three of them were arm-in-arm, sidestepping up the riverbed.

It was like walking through tar. Every step was a

herculean effort, made all the more difficult because of the need to synchronize with the other two, but they gradually worked their way upstream, passing under the place where they had broken through. The hole in the ceiling was dark and would stay that way until Bones returned. They kept going.

About fifty feet past that point, the cavern widened out considerably, which had the effect of making the river shallower—it was just ankle deep where they were standing—and significantly diminishing the power of the current. Maddock took a moment to savor the respite. "Okay," he said, "I think we can take our seat belts off and move about the cabin."

Slava stared back at him, bemused. "Seat belts?"

"I think he means we can let go of each other," Riddle explained, and then pointed to an odd shadow on the wall directly ahead. "Dane, check that out. Does that look like a cave?"

Maddock shone his light on the spot, which appeared to be a low recess, a couple feet wide, but rising only about eight inches above the waterline. "Could be," Maddock allowed. He moved cautiously toward it, and crouched down for a better look. "It looks like it's mostly underwater. Could be a tributary source for this river."

Riddle grinned. "Just mostly underwater?"

Maddock was curious despite himself. "I'll check it out, but if I run out of headspace, I'm turning around."

The opening was so low that moving forward required Maddock to low crawl on his belly through the shallow water, with his head turned to the side and angled up to keep mouth and nose above the surface. It was awkward but thankfully the ceiling lifted a few feet in, allowing him to push up onto his hands and knees. The floor of the passage rose also, until the water was merely a thin sheen rolling over and around the irregular rocks on its way down to the underground river.

Maddock crawled up the slight incline until there was enough headroom to rise into a crouch, and then he shone his headlamp into the surrounding darkness.

Something glinted back.

He scooted toward the reflection, half expecting it to be nothing more interesting than an exposed vein of iron pyrite, but as he neared it, he saw that it wasn't the mineral commonly called "fool's gold."

It was the real deal.

Real gold.

He knew the metal was gold without touching it, weighing it in his hands, or testing its relative softness, for one simple reason. The gold was not in a form usually found in nature—not dust, or nuggets, or even ore—but was rather in the shape of several disks, each about an inch or so in diameter.

Coins.

Dozens of them. Hundreds. The coins, and the rotted remains of the chest that had once contained them, were resting in a little nook that had been chiseled into the cave wall.

He picked up one of the coins, held it close for inspection. It was slightly irregular in shape and rather than being perfectly flat, was slightly cupped like a contact lens. Rather than heads and tails, both sides depicted stylized human figures, along with crosses and little symbols that might have been letters.

He set it back down, and then carefully removed the lid of the chest. Time and moisture had transformed the wood into something the consistency of soggy newspaper, and it fell apart in his hands, but not before revealing more coins, and something else.

It was a bowl, a little bigger than both his hands cupped together, and partially filled with coins. He began removing the latter with meticulous care, to expose the dark, faintly yellow patina of tarnished silver, and then teased the vessel out of the chest. It was slightly oblong, smooth almost all the way around its circumference, but on one side there were a pair of round indentations, a little more than an inch in diameter, and a little less than an inch apart, and into each, a dark red gemstone—probably a garnet—had been set. The exterior was studded with more cabochon cut gems—yellow, red, and green—and the wide-footed stem protruding from the bottom suggested that it was actually an oversized wine goblet.

Something about the shape and the set of the two garnets looked eerily familiar, and when he turned the cup upside down, his suspicions were confirmed.

The vessel had been fashioned to resemble the top half of an inverted, life-sized human skull.

"Guys," he shouted without looking back. "You should probably come in here."

5

"Do you realize what this means?" Riddle exclaimed as he stared down at Maddock's discovery.

Maddock could think of several answers to that question. "Well, for starters, I'd say it means there definitely is another way out of here."

Riddle waved a hand, dismissively. "Never mind that. It means that Nikolov was right."

"I don't follow. You said they weren't really looking for treasure. And don't tell me this is the remains of some extraterrestrial ancestor."

"Well, no. But you know how it can be with psychics. They get their wires crossed all the time. The things they see aren't always literal. Maybe he saw this skull and interpreted it as an ancestor."

Maddock pointed at the bowl. "That's not even a real skull."

"Actually, it is." Slava said. She did not sound or look very enthusiastic about the discovery. "This is the cup of Khan Krum."

The way she said the name reminded Maddock of the war god to which Conan the Barbarian had prayed before going into battle with the minions of Thulsa Doom.

"Who's that?" asked Riddle.

"Every school child in Bulgaria knows the story of Khan Krum. He was one of the greatest rulers of the First Bulgarian Empire, and a fearsome warrior who defeated the armies of the Byzantine emperor Nikephoros. When Nikephoros invaded Bulgaria, Krum attempted to negotiate, but Nikephoros did not want surrender. He only wanted to plunder and destroy. Burning cities and killing everyone. He even ordered children to be smashed with threshing stones. So, Krum raised an army of peasants… Even the women took up arms. They caught up with the Byzantine army at Vărbica Pass and wiped them out. Krum hung Nikephoros' severed head on a spear, and then when the flesh had rotted off the skull, he cut it open, lined it with silver, and made it into a cup for drinking wine. He would make his captured enemies drink from the cup to remind them what their fate would be if they did not submit." She pointed to the goblet. "That is the cup of Khan Krum, made from the skull of Nikephoros."

"You called him Khan Krum," Maddock "Not Tsar?"

"Krum was a Bulgar chieftain, not a Slav."

Maddock shook his head. "Sorry, I'm not clear on the difference."

"Bulgars were nomads from the east. They shared the Balkan peninsula with the Slavic tribes, and together forged the first empire. But they were always a minority among the Slavs, and after Krum's death, the Bulgars were gradually assimilated into the Slavic culture, and eventually converted to Christianity."

Maddock took another look at the cup. He didn't doubt that the lurid story Slava had just recounted was probably true, but it did not necessarily follow that, underneath a layer of tarnished silver, there was a human skull. "It's seems like a bit of a stretch to connect this cup to the ancient alien these psychics supposedly saw," he said. "But this is an amazing discovery nonetheless." He turned to Slava. "You'll definitely be able to get your own show after this."

Her pinched expression did not change. "We should not tell anyone of this," she said, a little hesitantly, and then to head off a protest from Riddle, added, "Not yet. Not until we get permission from the government."

"She's right," Maddock said. "The fewer people who know about this, the better. At least until we can move the treasure out of here and conduct a thorough survey of this cave system."

"We can start doing that right now," Riddle said.

Maddock shook his head. "I think we've all had enough adventure for one day. And Bones is probably wondering what happened to us."

"Let's at least take that with us." Riddle pointed to the skull cup. "It's the best part of this whole story, and I want to get it authenticated ASAP."

Maddock was inclined to veto the idea. "I have a feeling the authorities would rather have their archaeologists examine everything *in situ.*"

Slava however unexpectedly sided with Riddle. "We should take it with us."

Maddock spread his hands in a show of surrender. "If that's your decision as an official representative of the Bulgarian government, then who am I to argue?"

He carried the skull cup back through the passage, careful to keep it out of the water. Once they were all back in the main cave, they linked arms again and began a slow shuffle back toward the ledge where they had earlier rested, but no sooner had they started moving when a distinctive buzzing sound reached Maddock's ears. He glimpsed movement in the shadows and sought it out with the beam of his headlamp. It was Riddle's copter drone zipping toward them from the downriver section of the cave. It stopped about twenty feet away and hovered, its gimbal-mounted camera staring down.

Bones' voice boomed down from the opening in the ceiling. "Damn it, Maddock, what part of 'sit tight' did you not get? I was about ready to come down there after you."

"And leave Corey to anchor for you?"

"Naw, I figured out a better idea for that. I used the jack from Miss Bulgaria's Mercedes to rig up a bombproof anchor."

"Smart."

"Duh. Smarter than you taking off to go sightseeing."

Despite the distance between them, Maddock lowered his voice to what was almost a conspiratorial whisper. "Bones, we found something. Something big." He held up the silver cup. The drone shifted a little, as if trying to get a better look.

Bones stared down at him and shook his head. "First you don't even want to come here, then you hog all the fun, and leave me to pull your sorry ass out of trouble. Nice."

"Hey, we can trade places."

"Too late now," Bones said with an air of weary resignation. "Now, are you going to climb out of there, or do I have to pull you up?"

"I can climb," Maddock replied. "A rope would help. If it's not too much trouble."

"Screw you, Maddock," Bones fired back, but nevertheless dropped the end of the secured rope down through the hole. A pair of long rope loops, like handholds, were attached to the main line with prusik knots—a type of friction hitch that mountain climbers used to ascend fixed ropes. When there was no weight bearing down on the loop, the knot would easily slide up, but when it came under load, the hitch would lock down tight around the vertical line.

Maddock handed off the cup, and then took hold of the rope. An experienced climber, it took him only a few minutes to make his way up the hanging line by using the sliding loops as footholds. As he did, the drone continued to circle around him, catching the action from every conceivable angle. Maddock just shook his head. When he got to the top, Bones offered a hand to pull him the rest of the way out. Corey was there too, but he was wholly consumed with controlling the drone.

He figured Slava and Riddle would have a tougher time trying to prusik out, so instead of attempting to coach them on technique—and over Riddle's protests—he and Bones simply hauled them up the old-fashioned way.

The rest was anti-climatic. To preserve their secret a little longer, Maddock stuffed the skull cup inside an empty gear bag before emerging from the transformer shed, but this precaution proved unnecessary. Nobody in the little village had paid them the slightest attention.

While Maddock and Bones went about the task of stowing the climbing equipment, Corey set about making a three-dimensional scan of the cup. His plan, he explained, was to produce a full-scale replica using a 3-D printer, for use as a prop, just in case they needed to reshoot the moment of discovery at some point in the future. Riddle watched him work, on camera of course, and supplied additional commentary on their exploration of the Tsarichina Hole. In a hushed, almost reverential tone, the TV host played up the coincidences, such as the relative proximity of the treasure trove to the spot where the excavation had ended, and the possibility that the "ancestor" in Rumen's vision might have been a clouded perception of the physical remains of Emperor Nikephoros. Maddock did his best to ignore the monologue, but Bones was still hanging on Riddle's every word.

"I can't decide which is crazier," Bones said as he methodically coiled a hundred-foot section of rope. "The fact that the psychic dude zeroed in on the location of the treasure, or the fact that Bulgaria's frigging national hero cut off the head of his enemy and drank wine from his skull. That's so badass."

Riddle loudly shushed him, and then, after a moment's pause, resumed speaking.

"'Zeroed in' may be a bit of a stretch," Maddock countered, keeping his voice down.

"Are you kidding? Dude, you were right there. I mean sure, he got his signals crossed a little, but you can't deny that he got within spitting distance of a treasure that nobody even knew was there."

"And which he wasn't even looking for. This is like looking under the couch cushions for your keys and finding a couple bucks in loose change instead. It's serendipity, but you still don't have your keys. You don't get to call that a win."

"I think the whole 'first ancestor' thing might have been a smokescreen to throw looters and claim jumpers off the scent. I'll bet they were looking for treasure all along."

"Then why did they stop? I mean, if their psychic was so dialed in, why throw in the towel when they were so close?"

Bones had evidently been pondering this very question. "Max said they decided to call it quits when Baba Vanga warned them to stop. I've heard of this Baba Vanga chick before. She's like a modern Nostradamus. She predicted 9/11 in 1989. She said: 'The American brothers will fall after being attacked by the steel birds. The wolves will be howling in a bush.' Crazy, right?"

Maddock rolled his eyes. "Your point?"

"That cup is probably cursed. Maybe if you drink from it, you turn into a vampire or something. This *is* vampire country, you know. They have actual vampire hunters here who dig up dead people and stake them, just to make sure they don't come back."

"First aliens, and now vampires. What's next? Chupacabra?"

"Maybe the vampires *are* aliens," Bones persisted. "Did you ever consider that?"

Maddock shook his head. "You should be telling Max all this, not me."

"You're right." Bones tossed the tightly bound rope coil into the back of Slava's Mercedes. "We should probably be very careful with that skull, too. At least until we know what's going on with it."

"I have taken care of that," announced Slava, as she joined them, her mobile phone still in hand. Despite being back on the surface and done with "extreme sports" for the foreseeable future, she still seemed apprehensive about something. "I just spoke with Dr. Ivanova at the National Archaeological Institute. We are to deliver the cup of Khan Krum to her at the museum for authentication."

"Did you tell her where we found it?"

Slava nodded. "Not yet, but if it is authentic, she will want to know."

Bones cocked his head to the side. "Why did you just nod for 'no'?"

Slava's smile returned, if only for a few seconds. "Forgive me. I forgot. In Bulgaria, we nod for 'no', and shake our heads for 'yes.'"

"You're kidding?"

She nodded.

Bones started to nod as well, but then stopped. "Wait, what does that mean?"

6

"**I will get** your money," pleaded the little, fat man, squirming in a futile effort to protect his vulnerable mid-section. With his arms pinned behind him, the best he could manage was to raise his knees a few inches. "Please don't hurt me."

"Hurt you, Georgi?" replied Boyan Dragomirov. "Why would I do that? If I hurt you, you wouldn't be able to pay me what you owe. And you are going to pay, aren't you Georgi?"

"Yes. Yes. I will have it for you next week."

"Next week?" Boyan frowned, then pistoned his right fist into Georgi's exposed belly. The fat man's breath blew out in a whoosh, his mouth working like a beached fish. "I don't want the money next week, Georgi. I want it today. And right now, what I want is for you to tell me how…"

The buzz of his phone vibrating in his pocket distracted him in mid-threat. He took it out and glanced at the name and number indicated on the screen. He raised his eyes to the man holding Georgi immobile. "Nikolay. I think Georgi needs something to help him remember to pay his debts. Take care of it."

As a grinning Nikolay went to work, Dragomirov returned his attention to the still buzzing phone, thumbing the button to take the call. "Krasimir. What do you want? I'm busy right now."

"This is not Krasimir."

Dragomirov felt a tingle of apprehension. There was something strange about the voice—he couldn't tell if it was a man or woman speaking, and the cadence was unusual—but it was the mere fact that someone who was not his younger brother speaking from his brother's phone that made him uneasy. There might have been a perfectly good explanation for it, but his thoughts immediately went to the worst ones.

Had one of his rivals kidnapped Krasimir? Or worse, killed him?

"Who is this?" he said, cautiously.

"I am called Atanas."

The name rang a faint bell, but did not provide anything remotely resembling an answer. "Where is Krasimir? Let me talk to him."

"Your brother is not here."

The tingle was fast becoming an itch. "How did you get my brother's phone?" He said, grinding the question between his teeth.

"I do not have your brother's phone. I spoofed his number. Do you know what this word means?"

"Atanas," Dragomirov breathed into the phone. Now he recalled where he had heard the name. "You are the hacker."

He chose the word deliberately, knowing that someone with Atanas' reputation would find it offensive. The man—if it was a man—was one of a new breed of criminals who use technology the way Dragomirov and his associates used guns and cudgels. They stole money and information, even manipulated international markets, sabotaged computer systems and held them for ransom.

Atanas did not respond to the jab. "I would like to discuss a business proposition."

"Proposition? If you are trying to extort money from me—"

"If I wanted your money, I would simply take it. I can do that, you know. This is an opportunity for you."

Dragomirov tapped his fingers on the tabletop, struggling to switch mental gears. He was used to people approaching him with schemes to make money, and sometimes he listened, but cyber-crime was something he did not understand. He made it a point never to get involved with things he didn't understand. "I think you have the wrong man."

"You trade in unregulated antiquities, do you not?"

Dragomirov frowned. The black-market antiquities trade was his second most lucrative enterprise, after gambling. "Are you buying or selling?"

There was a long silence, as if Atanas was trying to decide how to answer the question. "This is a matter of acquisition."

"Ah, so you want something that is not for sale. You want it stolen. Go on. I'm listening."

"A very special artifact has been discovered. It is being taken to the National Museum for authentication."

"What is this special artifact?"

"The cup of Khan Krum."

Dragomirov sucked in a breath. "Truly? It has been found. Where?"

"That is not important. What is important is that you act quickly."

"The museum is like a fortress. Even I wouldn't try to steal from it."

"You misunderstand," Atanas said. "I do not want you to steal it. Here's what you must do."

7

Citing a desire for more legroom, Bones opted to ride in the backseat of Slava's Mercedes. Maddock suspected that was only one of his reasons why. Corey, almost guiltily, told Maddock he also wanted to ride with the others, "so I can get started downloading all this footage from the GoPros." All of which meant that Maddock had the little Fiat all to himself on the drive back to Sofia. The peace and quiet was a welcome relief. He didn't think he could handle half an hour of Bones speculating wildly about psychics, vampires and extraterrestrials.

Yet, despite his dismissal of the notion that the remote viewers had tuned in to something that had brought them within a stone's throw of an actual hidden treasure, Maddock was troubled by the coincidence. His father, who had spent years searching for the gold of Captain Kidd, once told him, "Someone will find it when it's ready to be found."

Sometimes, that was exactly what happened. Somebody would stumble across a valuable artifact in an attic, or find a cache of buried coins while excavating for the foundation of a house. But to find this particular treasure where they had, the way they had, almost demanded that he be open to unconventional ideas.

Usually, finding the treasure was the end of the mystery, but not this time. There were so many unanswered questions. Who hid the treasure in that remote cave? How did they get it there? When had they concealed it, and why?

He was looking forward to going back into the

Tsarichina Hole and exploring the cave system which intersected it. Perhaps they would discover the answers to those questions, but he doubted they would ever have a satisfactory solution to the puzzle of why the Tsarichina Hole had been excavated in the first place.

These thoughts kept him occupied during the relatively short drive back to Sofia. The landscape, mostly farm country, was pleasant if unremarkable, and gradually became more suburban as they neared the capital city. Slava navigated onto a narrow two-lane highway that seemed to skirt this divide for a while before finally plunging into the city proper. The drive ended on a wooded hilltop that seemed to float like an island amid the urban sea. Maddock parked the Fiat and went to join the others as they made their way up the long brick path that led to the National Historical Museum.

"That is one fugly museum," Bones remarked.

Slava cocked her head to one side. "I do not know this word."

Maddock sighed. Bones wasn't wrong about the museum. There was nothing visually appealing about the squat, rectangular structure that looked more like a post office or military command center than a museum. Even the sturdy-looking gate through which they had to pass to enter felt more like a defensive barrier than a crowd control measure.

"He just means it's got some interesting architecture," Maddock said quickly, hoping that Bones would get the hint.

"Right," Bones said, nodding slowly. "Interesting. That's the word for it. Kind of like when the best thing you can say about a chick is that she's got a great personality."

"This used to be the official residence of Chairman Zhivkov, the ruler of Bulgaria under Communist regime,"

Slava said.

"That explains why it looks so…" Maddock struggled to come up with a word.

"Fugly?" suggested Bones.

"The real treasures are inside," Slava promised. "Literally. Bulgaria has a long and very rich history."

They were met at the front entrance by a short, middle-aged woman wearing a white lab coat. She had close-cropped, steel-gray hair and a dour expression. Maddock didn't like to judge people too quickly, but his first impression of this woman was that she was not happy to see them. Her judgmental gaze seemed to linger on the duffel bag slung over Riddle's shoulder, as if she could see right through the nylon fabric.

Slava, switching between English and Bulgarian, took care of the introductions. The woman was Dr. Lyudmila Ivanova, head of the conservation and restoration department.

"Ask her if it's okay to record her," Riddle said to Slava.

"I wonder if the camera has a filter to reduce resting bitch face," Bones muttered.

"I speak English," Ivanova said, albeit with a thick accent. "I learned in high school."

Maddock winced, hoping that she hadn't heard Bones' comment.

"Great," Riddle replied, affably. "So can we?"

The woman's expression did not change appreciably. She turned to the attendant at the entrance desk and after a brief exchange, turned back and handed them all lanyards attached to plastic badges with Cyrillic writing. "You have permission to use your cameras, but you must wear these and keep them visible at all times."

When they had all looped the lanyards around their

necks, Ivanova indicated that they should follow her, and then set off into the museum. Corey, outfitted with a head-mounted GoPro, followed their progress through the museum, mostly focusing his attention on Riddle as the latter attempted to make small talk with their guide.

As Slava had indicated, the museum's brutalist façade concealed a lavish interior. Even without the displays—thousands of artifacts from more than seven millennia of the region's history—the marble and oak appointments made the building feel like a palace, which Maddock supposed it had been during the years when it had been occupied by Bulgaria's former dictator. As was too often the case in the Eastern bloc, the Communist leaders hid their own hypocritical bourgeoise excesses behind closed doors and bleak, constructivist walls.

But the real beauty was inside the glass display cases. Golden jewelry from the regions original Thracian inhabitants, Roman and Byzantine sculpture, manuscripts and icons from the Imperial periods. Maddock wished there had been time to explore the collection at length, but Ivanova set a brisk pace that did not allow time for sightseeing. Soon, they arrived an at unmarked door, which Ivanova opened holding her ID badge to the proximity card reader on the wall, and led them into a part of the museum that was off the public route.

The conservation laboratory was surprisingly bright and welcoming, with large windows that looked out on the park. Ivanova cleared a table and gestured to it. "So, let's see what you have brought me."

Riddle placed the duffel bag on the table and unzipped it, pulling it down to fully reveal the artifact inside. Ivanova drew in a sharp breath of surprise when she saw it, but then her face returned to its state of stern reserve. "I hope you did not touch it with bare hands," she said, taking a pair of white cotton gloves from the pocket of her lab coat.

"Sorry," Maddock said. "We weren't expecting to find anything."

"Is this the legendary cup of Khan Krum?" Riddle asked, clearly playing to the camera.

"It is too soon to tell," Ivanova replied, guardedly. She pulled on the gloves and then lifted the cup, turning it over in her hands. "We will have to run many tests. But it is very interesting piece. Where did you find it?"

"We are not ready to reveal that just yet," Slava said. "But I assure you, as soon as it is authenticated, we will turn everything over to the proper authorities."

Ivanova seemed less than happy with that response, but did not press the matter. Instead, she bent down close to the cup and began scrutinizing it millimeter by millimeter.

"I'd like to follow you through the authentication process," Riddle said. "What's your schedule look like?"

Ivanova sucked in a breath and stood up abruptly. "This is not right. There is writing here." She pointed to the cup's interior. The letters were barely visible in the tarnished metal, and Maddock had to strain his eyes to see them, but they were definitely there.

"It is Bulgarian," Ivanova added.

"Imagine that," Bones remarked.

Ivanova shook her head. "The language of Bulgaria… the written language… was created by Saints Cyril and Methodius in the mid-Ninth Century, and first used in Bulgaria. The reign of Khan Krum ended in AD 814, eighty years before the Cyrillic alphabet was first used. That original language was called Old Bulgarian, or sometimes, Old Church Slavonic. It was not the language of Krum the Bulgar."

"I think I get it," Maddock said. "It's like reading Chaucer in the original Middle English. It's English, but it's almost unintelligible."

Ivanova nodded again, which Maddock had to remind himself meant the opposite of what he thought it did. "Modern Bulgarian—the form we use today—was introduced in the Sixteenth Century. That is what is written here. This engraving cannot be from the time of Krum. I would say, at the earliest, it is only five hundred years old. But probably much more recent than that."

"What does it say?" Bones asked.

Ivanova turned her irritated gaze on him for a moment, then returned her attention to the cup. "It says, '*Namerete istinski bogat·stva, kŭdeto Bog vi nablyudava.*'"

"Look for treasure where God watches over you," said Slava, translating.

"Something like that," Ivanova said, and then, added almost dismissively, "it is common Christian sentiment. Wealth cannot bring salvation. Only the blood of Christ can do that, so it is the real treasure. But Khan Krum was not Christian."

"That doesn't necessarily mean it isn't Krum's cup," Riddle said, sounding a little defensive. "Couldn't somebody have added the inscription later?"

"It is possible," she admitted, but with more than a little skepticism. "We will know more when we have completed tests. If there is a skull under the silver, we can carbon date it. Possibly even extract enough DNA to determine ethnicity. Until we can do the tests, there really isn't anything more I can tell you."

There was a note of finality in her reply, and Maddock sensed that any further inquiries would put a strain on their working relationship with the scientist. Before Riddle could repeat his request for access to the authentication process, Maddock spoke up. "We should let you get to it then." He turned to Riddle. "I don't know about you, but I could stand a hot shower, a change of clothes, and something to eat."

Slava shook her head. "Yes, that is what we should do. I will take you to your hotel so you can get cleaned up, and then I will take you all out to dinner. I know the perfect place."

"As long as there's beer," Bones said, "I'm in."

Riddle looked like he was about to protest, but Ivanova seized control of the moment. "Good. I will contact you when I have more information."

She hurried them back to the entrance where they surrendered their visitor's passes. A few minutes later, they were back in their respective vehicles. Maddock once more flew solo in the Fiat, following Slava's M-Class through the city on a busy expressway.

Judging from what he saw passing by his windows, Sofia appeared to be a modern city, but Maddock knew that the view, like the expressway, was just the latest layer of a history going back several millennia.

He was a little surprised at the prevalence of English on the signage he passed—yet another indicator of Sofia's emergence into the Twenty-First Century and the global market. The hotel Slava led him to was an international chain; its familiar logo was in English, as was the name of the adjoining business—Princess Casino.

Bones will love that, he thought.

Sure enough, as Maddock approached the reception desk at the hotel, Bones' voice boomed across the lobby. "Yo, dude. Can you believe this place? There are like fifteen casinos, just in Sofia. Why didn't we come here sooner?"

"Maybe because we like keeping our hard-earned

cash?" Maddock retorted.

Bones rolled his eyes. "Maybe you like *keeping* it. I like doubling it."

"You sound like your uncle," Maddock said. Bones' uncle, "Crazy" Charlie Bonebrake, owned several casinos.

Slava, who had just finished checking them in, approached them and handed each man an envelope containing a room key card. "Your friend Corey is helping Max unload the equipment," she said, and then turned to Maddock. "I take it you are not a gambler, Mr. Maddock?"

"I'll play nickel slots once in a while, but no, not like him." He nodded his head in Bones' direction.

"I would have thought that treasure hunting and gambling have a lot in common."

"Maybe for some," Maddock admitted. "But I'm not chasing the big jackpot. I've always been more interested in exploring the past and solving old mysteries."

She smiled, but somehow it didn't quite reach her eyes. "Maybe you will get lucky and solve the mystery of the Tsarichina Hole."

"I'll certainly give it my best shot," Maddock answered, but in that moment, the mystery that he was most curious about was the abrupt change in Slava's demeanor. It was almost as if she didn't want him to make good on that promise.

8

Two hours later, feeling considerably cleaner and drier, and only a little jet-lagged, Dane Maddock stepped from his hotel room and walked down the hall to Bones' room. When his knock went unanswered, he moved to Corey's door.

Although he had managed to avoid getting soaked in the subterranean river below Tsarichina, Corey actually looked a little worse for wear. He passed a hand through his thinning red hair. "Oh, sorry. I lost track of the time. I've been going over all the camera footage, trying to cut it together. It's going to make a great show."

"Well, you can finish the post-production later," Maddock said. "We're supposed to meet the others downstairs in five minutes."

Corey nodded, and then quickly stripped off his rumpled T-shirt, applied a coat of Degree to his armpits, and then pulled on a fresh shirt from his still unpacked suitcase.

"Have you seen Bones?" Maddock asked. "I knocked, but he didn't answer."

"Are you seriously asking?" Corey said, laughing. "He's been downstairs at the casino pretty much since we got here."

Maddock rolled his eyes. "Of course he has."

"He invited me to join him, but I wanted to get started on the video."

As Corey finished changing, Maddock took out his phone and fired off a text to Bones.

Did you double yet?

The reply came back within seconds.

Screw you, Maddock.

Maddock laughed. *Meet you downstairs in five.*

Riddle and Slava were waiting for them in the hotel lobby. He was attired in a clean version of the outfit he always wore on his show—a light beige photojournalist-style shirt, brown cargo pants, and hiking boots, while their Bulgarian hostess had donned a sleeveless floral print cocktail dress and stiletto heels. Her cheerful demeanor was also once more in evidence, and she greeted both Maddock and Corey with a hug.

"You got taller," Maddock remarked as they embraced.

"It's the shoes," she fairly chirped. "Do you like them?"

She took a step back and then executed a half-turn, like a runway model, striking a pose. Maddock didn't know much about shoes, but the three-inch heels accentuated her already shapely calves. "Very nice," he said, and then wondered if that was the correct response.

"Where's Bones?" Riddle asked.

"Where do you think?" Corey replied, jerking a thumb toward the entrance that led to the casino.

"Guess again, numbnuts," Bones said as he approached from the elevator lobby behind them. Maddock thought his friend looked a little out of breath, and guessed his text message had prompted Bones to pull off a superhero-quick costume change. That he'd managed to make it back up to his room, changed into a fresh shirt, and then made it back down to the lobby in less than five minutes was an impressive feat. As he joined the group, Bones regarded Slava with barely concealed lasciviousness.

He looked like he was about to say something, but before he could, Slava stepped toward him and gave him a hug, which seemed to totally throw him off his game.

"Oh, look at that," he managed to say. "You're a hugger."

The embrace ended as quickly as it had begun, and then Slava addressed them all. "The restaurant is only about a mile away. We can take the tram. It will be easier than trying to find parking, and I can show you some sights along the way."

"There's a perfectly good restaurant right there," Bones countered, nodding toward the casino entrance.

Slava waved a dismissive hand. "I'm sure you will have plenty of chances to eat there, but I want to take you somewhere special."

"Sounds good," Maddock said. "Lead the way."

The tram rail line ran down the street to the east of the hotel. Slava led them south about half a block to a sheltered stand where a few other people were waiting. A few minutes later, a very modern-looking yellow light-rail streetcar pulled up. After confirming that it was the line they wanted—the number 18—Slava handed out tickets and then stepped up into the tram where she demonstrated how to use the automated ticket validation device located by the doors.

The tram had an open design, with single, forward facing seats on either side, and plenty of standing room in the center. The car wasn't crowded by any means, but Slava elected to stand, so Maddock and the others did, too.

As the tram rolled down the street, Maddock saw a very different city from what he had beheld on the expressway drive. The buildings looked older, especially once they crossed a bridge adorned with lion sculptures.

"There is Sofia Synagogue," Slava called out as they

crossed an intersection right after leaving from their second stop along the route. She pointed down the street to their right, where an immense domed structure was just barely visible. "And ahead on the left, is the Banya Bashi mosque. It was built in the Sixteenth Century, when Bulgaria was ruled by the Ottoman Empire."

The mosque was not large, but it was distinctive, with a silvery-gray dome, peaked arches, and a tall brick minaret.

"And right there," Slava went on, pointing to a sunken area in the foreground, just beyond the sidewalk, "are the ruins of old Serdica, the Roman city that was once here. Constantine the Great built a palace here, and even considered making Serdica the capital of the Eastern Empire instead of Byzantium. This part of the excavation is open to the public. I think you would especially like the place, Mr. Maddock."

He was about to tell her to just call him by his first name, but Bones jumped in. "What made this place so special?"

Slava smiled. "The Romans, as you probably know, loved hot baths. There are several hot springs here. Sofia is still famous for its hot mineral water. Back there, in the park behind the mosque, there are fountains where the hot water pours out. Many Bulgarians come and fill containers with it to use at home. It is supposed to have special healing properties."

Bones rolled his eyes. "Probably tastes like crap."

She nodded. "It doesn't really have any flavor. Of course, you have to let it cool before you can drink it. The water is very hot when it comes out." Slava paused, as if she had run out of things to say, then pointed in the opposite direction. "Over there is the monument to the city's namesake, Sveta Sofia."

Maddock swung his gaze around, expecting to see some kind of ancient statue or weathered monolith, but instead saw a modern-looking metal sculpture of a woman, standing on a high pedestal, towering above a small park. The statue's skin was bright brass, as was the crown atop her head, but everything else was dark bronze. Her arms were outstretched as if in welcome. In her right hand, she held a wreath, and an owl was perched on her left shoulder. She wore a cryptic expression, and her eyes, which looked like black hollows in her face, were almost creepy.

"Must be cold up there," Bones remarked. "She should put on a sweater."

Maddock grimaced as he realized what Bones was talking about. Beneath her sculpted bronze gown, Sveta Sofia had very prominent, erect nipples.

"I expected something a little older," Maddock said quickly, before Bones could supply additional explicit commentary. "That looks pretty modern."

"It was put up in 2000," Slava said. "There used to be a statue of Lenin there, but it was removed when the Communists lost power. You can still see it though in the Museum of Socialist Art."

The street curved a little, removing the rather suggestive statue from their view as the tram came to another stop.

"Over there," Slava said, redirecting their attention to the opposite side of the street, "Is the Largo Complex and the Hotel Balkan. The Largo houses several government offices, including the Presidency. In the inner courtyard however is the oldest building in Sofia—the Church of St. George. It was part of the old Roman city, built in the time of Constantine. It is very beautiful inside.

"And that," she went on, pointing to the ornate, free-standing structure adjacent to the hotel, "is Saint Nedelya Cathedral Church. The original church was built in the Tenth Century, but it has been rebuilt many times. This structure was completed in 1933. You can't quite see it from here, but Sofia's most famous landmark, the Saint Alexander Nevsky Cathedral, is about half a kilometer away. If you want, you can visit all of them in a day, on foot."

The Alexander Nevsky Cathedral had come up in Maddock's Google search of things to do in Sofia, as had the fact that Nevsky was not Bulgarian. "Why is your most famous landmark named for a Russian prince?"

"The name was chosen to honor Russian soldiers who died to liberate Bulgaria from Ottoman rule."

"Another dome," said Corey. "What is it with religious buildings and domes?"

"It's not dome," Bones said, altering his voice slightly as if trying to do an impression—of whom, Maddock couldn't say. "It's 'do me.' 'Do.' 'Me.' Two separate words."

Maddock rolled his eyes. "If that's supposed to be some kind of reference…" He waved his hand over his head. "Whoosh."

Corey however seemed to be on the same wavelength as Bones, and chimed in a similarly affected voice. "Big hit. Bell Biv DeVoe." He laughed. "Oh, man. Richard Cheese. I forgot about that."

Maddock sighed. "I think it's going to be a long night."

Riddle laughed. "I love you guys. We should be filming this."

"Why, are you trying to land a gig on Comedy Central now?"

"Nah. But lighthearted banter is good for ratings."

Maddock looked over to Bones and Corey. "Did you

hear that, guys? Save it for when the cameras are rolling."

A tone sounded, signaling that the doors were about to close, and the tram began moving again. It curled around the front of the Nedelya Cathedral, and then continued south for a couple blocks before taking a hard left turn. It continued east for a block, and then angled to the southeast.

"This is our stop," Slava said, stepping toward the door. "The restaurant is just a couple blocks away."

After they disembarked, Slava led them to the next intersection and turned right, heading west down a narrow one-way street. After the wide-open thoroughfare which the tram had shared with auto traffic, this street felt almost claustrophobic.

A short ways down, they took another turn, this time to the south, and continued on past residential entrances and storefronts until they reached the entrance to an establishment that seemed like the very definition of the expression "hole in the wall." An old-fashioned hay cart, painted with a colorful folk art pattern, hung suspended above the door, and protruding from it was a carved wooden sign. Maddock couldn't read the Cyrillic letters, but the bottom line was in English: "Restaurant."

"This is Hadjidragonov's Cellars," Slava said. "It is very popular with tourists. Best place to get traditional Bulgarian food."

Maddock decided to reserve judgement on the food, but he could see why it was a popular destination for visitors. The interior looked like a cross between a museum of Bulgarian culture and a carnival funhouse. As the name suggested, the prevailing theme was of an old village wine cellar, and the main hall was decorated with several polished wooden barrels, along with various *objets d'art*. The overall effect was a little kitschy. A trio of musicians—playing drum, accordion, and flute, respectively— were performing in the center of the room. They were attired in what Maddock surmised were traditional Bulgarian costumes: loose fitting, collarless shirts with red, green, and gold embroidered floral patterns running up the sleeves; embroidered vests of red and green; light-colored trousers with, of course, embroidery running along the outside seams; and embroidered gaiters. Two of the men wore conical hats with red and white feather plumes, and all three were sporting impressive mustaches. The tune reminded Maddock of traditional Greek music, and while he wasn't particularly keen to hear more, he admired the gusto with which they played.

"Oh, yeah," Bones lamented, raising his voice almost to a shout. "This is so much better than the casino restaurant. Very intimate."

"Oh, come on," said Riddle. "This is great."

"We can sit in the garden," Slava said. "It's a little quieter."

They passed through the establishment and outside the rear door to an open courtyard where dozens of tables sat under the shade of capacious patio umbrellas. They found a table that was as far from the noise of the interior as they could manage. Because several of the dishes required a great deal of advanced preparation, Slava had placed their food order when making the reservations, and so shortly after delivering their first round of drinks the waitress brought over an enormous tray filled with skewers, sausages, various cuts of meat, sauces, dips, roasted vegetables, cheeses, and bread. Some of it was delicious, and some of it, as was often the way with so-called delicacies, was incomprehensibly vile. Maddock, Bones, and Corey washed theirs down with Stella Artois beer, while Slava and Riddle split a bottle of Bulgarian Gewürztraminer.

More dishes followed, along with a few more rounds of drinks. The food reminded Maddock of Greek and Mediterranean fare. Quite a bit of it involved lamb, which Maddock didn't usually care for, but the yogurt and eggplant sauces were delicious.

With their appetites largely sated, the focus shifted to conversation. Corey brought out his tablet and began showing Riddle some of the raw footage he had downloaded from the cameras. Despite having lived through most of it, Maddock was curious to see if the cameras had recorded anything that had escaped his notice. Bones let out a low whistle when the video revealed the moment where Maddock first beheld the treasure.

"So what do we think the story is here?" he wondered aloud. "Who put that treasure there? And why?"

"Why does anyone hide treasure?" Maddock countered. "They want to keep it safe until they need it. They plan to come back for it, but then something bad happens and they never do."

"That's the why, but what about the who? If Professor Grumpy-face is right, then that treasure was put there a long time after this guy Krum turned his enemy into stemware."

"Let's assume that the cup was handed down through several generations before it ended up in that treasure trove," Maddock said. "That makes the question of who a lot less important. Never mind when."

"What about that inscription?" Corey said. "It talked about looking for treasure, didn't it?" He fiddled with the tablet a moment, and then brought up the segment of video where Slava translated the Bulgarian inscription.

Look for treasure where God watches over you.

Corey paused the playback. "Wouldn't that mean there's more treasure?"

Slava gave a contrary nod. "You heard what Dr. Ivanova said. It is a spiritual message."

"But what if it's not," Bones speculated. "What if it's talking about literal treasure? Maybe that chest full of gold coins is only the tip of the iceberg."

Maddock turned to Slava. "Are there any stories about Krum having a lost treasure?"

"There are many stories of treasure," Slava said. "Bulgarians love searching for it. It is a national pastime. And unfortunately, much of what is found is sold on the black market. But most are looking for the gold of Tsar Samuil or Ivan Shishman."

Maddock glanced over at Riddle. "Samuil. You mentioned him earlier."

Riddle nodded. "When the dig at Tsarichina started, everyone thought they were looking for his treasure."

"Corey, go to the part where we found the coins," Maddock said. "If we can identify what time period these coins came from, it would at least give us a secondary point of reference."

Corey bent over the tablet, and after a few seconds of searching, isolated a frame where the coins were most prominent. He tapped and swiped the image, and then opened a web browser. After several minutes of opening and closing pages that displayed all manner of coinage, he announced, "I think this is a match. It's a coin from the Byzantine Empire, called a *histamenon*." He read a few more lines then went on. "Specifically, a histamenon from the reign of Constantine VIII, who ruled in the early Eleventh Century."

"That would have been about the same time as Tsar Samuil," Slava supplied.

"So the coins are Byzantine, not Bulgarian?" asked Bones.

"Byzantium was the major empire of the day," answered Maddock. "Their currency would have been in use all over the region."

Slava shook her head in agreement. "That is correct. I don't believe Samuil ever minted his own coinage."

Riddle spoke up. "You said Eleventh Century. That would be a couple hundred years after Krum, right?"

Slava shook her head once.

"What else can you tell us about Samuil?" Maddock asked.

"He was a great military leader," said Slava. "He was general of the armies of Tsar Roman I, the last ruler of Krum's dynasty. Roman spent most of his reign as a hostage in Constantinople, so Samuil was already the de facto ruler of Bulgaria, but when Roman died, he ascended the throne. Under his reign, the territory of the Bulgarian Empire extended throughout the Balkans. He was said to be invincible in battle, though later in life, he suffered many defeats, the worst of which was the Battle of Kleidion. At the end, he was surrounded by his enemies. Four years after his death, the first Bulgarian Empire ceased to exist."

"What happed to his body?" Corey asked. "Was there a royal tomb or anything like that?"

"Samuil's remains were interred at the Church of St. Achillios," replied Slava. "At the time, that was part of his empire, but today it is part of Greece. To the best of my knowledge, he was buried according to the tradition of the Church."

"So no grave goods like King Tut," said Bones. "But that doesn't mean he didn't have a stash of treasure. Think about it. That cup was probably handed down to Krum's descendants. When that Roman dude died, it would have gone to Samuil, along with the rest of the royal treasury. And maybe, after getting his ass handed to him at that battle, he decided to hide the treasure so his enemies wouldn't get their hands on it. Jump forward a few hundred years… Someone finds the treasure, takes part of it to Tsarichina, and hides the rest."

"Why would this hypothetical treasure hunter only take part of it?"

Bones shrugged. "Maybe he was afraid of drawing too much attention to himself. Who knows? But we do know that someone left a message in that cup, talking about treasure."

"If it is talking about real treasure," Maddock said, "and not just something symbolic, what does the clue mean?"

Slava's forehead creased as if in response to an unpleasant thought.

"You just had an idea," Maddock prompted.

"It is probably nothing," she replied, hesitantly. "'Where God watches' could be referring to Prohodna. It is a cave, about a hundred kilometers from Sofia. It is also called 'Eyes of God Cave' because there are two eye-shaped holes in the roof."

"I take it Bulgarians have known about this cave for quite a while?"

Slava shook her head. "For as long as people have lived here. Since prehistoric times." Then she nodded. "But it is a very popular place. If there was a treasure there, somebody would have found it already."

"Maybe there's another clue on the cup. One we didn't see," Bones suggested.

"On it," Corey said, and began swiping pages on his tablet. "I actually combined all this into a CAD file and ordered a 3-D print. It should be ready by tomorrow morn… Okay, here it is." He placed the tablet flat on the table so that everyone could see it. "I punched it up a little to make it easier to see."

Instead of a static photograph, the screen showed the cup slowly rotating, giving the illusion of a three-dimensional object. It was far from perfect, but the changing perspectives and visual enhancements almost made the cup seem more real than when Maddock had first beheld it.

He reached out a finger and tapped the screen, which froze the image. Clearly visible in Corey's hi-def image was a jagged seam with several short branch-like extensions, which crossed the interior of the cup.

"What's this squiggly line?"

"Skull sutures," Bones said. "The skull is made up of several different bones that fuse together during fetal development. The lines where they join are called skull sutures." He realized everyone was looking at him, and added. "What? I've dated a lot of nursing students. They like it when I help them study anatomy and physiology."

"TMI," Maddock said, rolling his eyes, then returned to the picture on the tablet. "I think it's supposed to look like a skull suture, but it's not in the right position."

Bones took another look, and then nodded in agreement. "You're right. Maybe the Emperor dude suffered a severe head trauma when he was a kid."

"Or maybe it's another clue," Corey said. "Or a map."

Everyone took another look.

Riddle was the first to put it all together. "So you think maybe if we go to this Eyes of God cave, the map will show us how to find the rest of the treasure."

Maddock raised his hands. "Let's not get ahead of ourselves."

Riddle shook his head. "No, let's. This is how great television is made, Dane. We'll drive out to this cave tomorrow and poke around. Even if we don't find anything, we'll have some great footage."

"Sounds good to me," Bones said. He grabbed his half-empty bottle of Stella and raised it to the center of the table. "To making great television!"

Maddock joined the toast, albeit with some reservations. The inscription and strange lines inside the bowl of the skull cup seemed to hint at the potential for more treasure, but he wasn't a fan of Riddle's incautious, damn-the-torpedoes approach to searching for it. Besides, there was plenty of treasure waiting to be recovered from the cave where they'd found the cup. Looking for one that might or might not exist seemed foolhardy.

Still, the visit to Bulgaria was turning out to be a lot more interesting than he'd expected.

Despite nearly unanimous protestations of being too stuffed for even a wafer-thin mint, Slava insisted on ordering a sampling of desserts. Maddock was already regretting his overindulgence both with respect to food and alcohol. He wasn't drunk, but he felt slow and sluggish. He declined even a bite of dessert, as did Bones. Corey and Riddle managed only a small bite of each item, after which Slava asked the waitress to package the items for takeaway. With the bill paid, they headed back through the boisterous interior of the restaurant, and made their way toward the exit.

As they were about to step out however, a young man wearing a stained white apron intercepted them. He spoke in halting English. "Excuse me, please, but are you *Maximum Mysteries*?"

Riddle grinned. "I'm the host of the show."

"Chef is big fan. Would like to photograph with you."

"Is he? That's wonderful. Yes, of course. I'd love to meet him."

The young man gestured to a door behind him. "This way. Please."

Riddle offered an apologetic shrug to his companions. "Sorry, guys. Can't disappoint the fans. Be right back."

As the TV host followed the young man toward the kitchen, Slava called after him, "We'll wait outside."

Maddock was glad to hear that, and with the others, followed her out of the noisy restaurant.

The street was quiet by comparison, though there was a fair amount of pedestrian traffic. After a few seconds of waiting in silence, Maddock looked over at Bones. "So are you gonna hit the casino again or call it a night?"

Bones stroked his chin thoughtfully, then looked over at Slava. "I don't know. I guess it depends on whether Lady Luck is sitting at my side."

Slava, who was looking down at her phone, did not appear to register the veiled invitation. With no response forthcoming, Bones shrugged and turned back to Maddock. "How about you? Want to try living a little, or have you got a date with a Metamucil nightcap and an empty bed?"

"Screw you," Maddock replied, albeit a little half-heartedly.

"Count me out," Corey said. "I'm gonna keep working on the video."

"You better make sure Max pays you."

Corey laughed. "I'll settle for a producer credit."

Maddock shook his head, then glanced back at the restaurant entrance. "What's taking him so long?"

"Maybe we should go in there and drag him out," Bones suggested.

Before Maddock could respond, Slava held up her phone to show them Riddle's name and photo on the screen. "He's calling me." She thumbed the button to receive the call and held it to her ear. "Max, what's taking—"

She stopped speaking abruptly, her face creasing in a look of confusion that quickly gave way to concern.

Maddock felt a tingling sensation run up his spine. Something was wrong. A surge of adrenaline washed away his sluggishness, putting him instantly on full alert. He shot a glance in Bones' direction, and wasn't surprised to see that the big man was already moving, dashing back into the restaurant to find their friend.

Maddock turned his attention back to Slava. "What is it?" he asked, and then, without waiting for an answer or permission, he snatched the phone from her hand and held it to his ear. The voice issuing from the speaker was most definitely not Riddle. Maddock couldn't tell if it was male or female, and guessed, based on the almost monotone delivery that it was an electronically generated voice. He didn't understand the words which he assumed were in Bulgarian, but took a chance and barked, "Who is this?"

The voice stopped. A brief silence ensued, during which time Maddock strained to catch any audible clues in the background, but there was nothing. Not even static. A moment later the same voice repeated his question back in unaccented English. "Who is this?"

"You first," Maddock said. "Where's Max?"

There was a momentary pause, and then, "You must be Mr. Maddock. I have your friend. He is safe, but if you ever want to see him again, you must follow my instructions."

9

Maddock's heart was racing. His pulse pounded in his head, roaring like a waterfall in his ears. Riddle had been abducted. Kidnapped practically right in front of them.

He searched his memory, trying to recall the techniques he had learned in SEAL training for dealing with a situation like this—a captured comrade, a negotiation. Most of the training had been focused on how to survive and escape capture, not what to do when someone else was the victim of an abduction.

The one thing he did remember was time and location were critical factors. Very little of the former had passed, which meant Riddle's kidnappers had to be close by. Maybe still in an alley outside the restaurant. Unfortunately, with each passing second, the circle of uncertainty about Riddle's location would grow in size. Bones might get lucky enough to catch them in the act of departing, but Maddock doubted the hostage-takers would have made the call if they were still on the premises.

That left it to him to open negotiations.

As these thoughts flashed through his head, the voice continued speaking. "First, do not contact the authorities. I will know if you do, and I promise, you will never see your friend again. Do you understand?"

Maddock weighed his options. So far, the kidnapper was practically reading from the standard script. Next would come the ransom demand. Agreeing to anything, even the order to refrain from contacting the authorities, would give the kidnappers all the power in whatever negotiations followed. Maddock's first impulse was to simply hang up and refuse to engage. Experience told him that the odds of Riddle surviving, even if the ransom was paid, were not good, but a refusal to engage with the kidnappers might make them simply cut their losses and either turn Riddle loose before things went too far, or simply kill him.

Maddock couldn't take that chance. Riddle's best chance for survival lay with Maddock and Bones tracking down the kidnappers and rescuing him, and to do that, he had to keep the lines of communication open. The kidnappers had used Riddle's phone to make this call, and if they continued to do so, tracking them would be a piece of cake.

"Yes," he finally answered. "I understand. Now, what do you want? If it's money you're after, then I'm afraid you're talking to the wrong person."

"I do not want money. You found something today. That is what I want."

Because he had been expecting a monetary demand, it took Maddock a second or two to process. "I'm sorry, what?"

"The cup of Khan Krum. You found it. I want it."

"I don't have it," Maddock protested. "We turned it over to someone at the museum."

The kidnapper's reply came immediately. "Then you will have to get it back."

"It's not that simple."

"It is simple. Get the cup. *How*, is your problem. I will trade your friend, Mr. Riddle, for the cup of Khan Krum. I will contact you again in twenty-four hours with instructions for the exchange. That is how long you have. There will be no extensions. And let me emphasize again, if you contact the authorities, you will never see Max Riddle again."

"What if I need to—" A double-beep tone in Maddock's ear signaled that the caller had terminated the connection. Maddock bit back a curse and then thrust the phone toward Corey who stared back at him in confusion. "Max has been kidnapped," Maddock said in a low voice.

"Kidnapped?" Corey gasped.

Slava shook her head once, in confirmation.

"Can you track his phone?" Maddock pressed. "Get a location?"

"Sure," Corey nodded, and then handed the phone back to Slava. "I don't need this. Just his number." He paused a moment before adding, "Of course, the kidnappers must know that. If they haven't already destroyed his phone, it would be a miracle."

"Just do what you can."

"What do they want?" Slava asked. "I heard you mention the museum."

"They want the cup. Beats me how they even knew about it in the first place. Someone at the museum must have leaked the fact that we brought it in."

"That makes no sense," Corey challenged. "If they know the cup is at the museum, why grab Max? It's out of our hands."

"I tried telling them that." Maddock glimpsed Bones returning from his dash to the kitchen.

The big man was scowling angrily, and as he reached them, he shook his head. "Long gone. And wouldn't you know it, everybody forgot how to speak English. I take it they got Max?"

Maddock nodded.

"So who are they?"

"Good question, but let's not talk about it here." Maddock gestured to the street. "Let's go."

This time, when they made their way up the street,

there was no conversation or languorous sightseeing. Maddock and Bones bracketed Corey and Slava, like bodyguards escorting their charges through a potentially hostile environment. Instead of returning to the tram, Maddock directed Slava to hail a taxi to take them directly back to the hotel.

When they got there, Maddock surprised everyone by suggesting they confer in the casino lounge, rather than meet in the privacy of a hotel room. When they had settled in at a table and placed their beverage orders—which in this case consisted of soft drinks only—Maddock explained his reasoning.

"I don't know if it's safe to speak openly in the hotel rooms," he explained. "It will be a lot harder for anyone to surveil us in here."

"Makes sense," Corey agreed. "Though I can rig up an RF scanner and sweep the room for bugs."

"Do that. But there are a lot of ways to eavesdrop that don't involve radio frequencies, so let's mind what we say up there."

"You really think the kidnappers are keeping tabs on us?" Bones asked.

"They knew where to find us tonight. We have to assume they are." He turned to Slava. "Do you have any idea who might be behind this?"

She pursed her lips together as if she knew the answer but was afraid to say it out loud. Finally, she overcame her fear. "There are criminals in Bulgaria—we call them *mutri*. You would call them mafia."

"Organized crime."

She shook her head once. "They are very powerful, with a great deal of influence in the government. There is a saying, 'Other countries have the mafia. In Bulgaria, the mafia has the country.' They have police and government officials in their pocket. If you were to go to the police about this, they would know."

"Why would the mafia want Max?" Corey wondered.

"The real question," said Maddock, "Is what would the mafia want with that cup?"

"The *mutri* do trade in illegal antiquities," offered Slava. "And if it is the cup of Khan Krum, then it would be almost priceless, especially to a Bulgarian collector."

"Do you think maybe they know that it's a treasure map?" asked Corey.

"Dude," Bones said, "*We* don't even know that it's a treasure map. That's just speculation."

"And we only just figured out that it might be," Maddock added.

"If they were watching us at the restaurant, maybe they overheard. Maybe that's why they decided to make a move."

Bones shook his head. "None of that matters. We need to focus on getting Max back. How are we going to do that?"

Maddock had been trying to figure that out ever since the phone call. "We don't have a lot of options here. We can't go to the police, and we don't have the cup, so we can't pay the ransom."

"We can get the cup back," Slava said. "We can tell Dr. Ivanova that it was a fake. A publicity stunt that Max cooked up for the show."

Bones shrugged. "It might work."

"And if it doesn't?" Maddock countered.

Bones snapped his fingers and pointed at Corey. "You said you're making a 3-D replica of the cup, right? What if we gave that to the kidnappers instead? The old switcheroo."

"A 3-D print isn't an exact replica," Corey said. "For

one thing, it's made of polymer, not silver. It would be pretty obvious that it wasn't the real deal."

"We'd only need to fool them long enough to make the exchange."

"We have to give them the real cup," Slava said. "We can't take chances with Max's life."

"There's no guarantee that they'll let him go even if we do give them what they want," Maddock said. "But I agree. We'll do what we can to try and figure out where they're hiding Max, but we need to get our hands on that cup before the deadline."

"Okay," Bones said, "who's going to volunteer to try and convince Professor Sourpuss that we made the whole thing up. Sorry for wasting your time, but could you do us a solid and give it back? I nominate Maddock."

Maddock shook his head again. "We're not going to ask for it back. We're going to steal it."

Everyone stared at him in disbelief. Bones was first to break the silence. "Dude, I'm the one who's supposed to come up with dumbass ideas like that."

"I don't see that we have a choice. But if we do this right, we'll use the drop to identify the kidnappers. Once Max is safe, we'll make sure the cup is returned to the museum."

"Oh, that's not the part of this cockamamie plan that bothers me. It's the stealing part."

"I figured you could handle that."

Bones folded his arms across his chest. "Oh, I see how it is. If you need something stolen, get the Indian to do it. It's in his blood."

"Oh, come on."

"No, it's cool," Bones said. "I mean, it's totally not cool that you're racist, but it's obvious that I'm the only one here who has got the requisite skills to pull off a heist like this."

"Actually, that's not quite true," Maddock said. "This isn't going to be your garden variety break-in. That museum has a lot of valuable stuff in it, and that means security is going to be tight." He swung his gaze to Corey. "Are you up for it?"

Corey's face went blank. "Me?"

"We know exactly where we need to go, and thanks to you filming our visit, we've got enough for a virtual walkthrough. Bones and I will do the actual legwork, but we're going to need you to hack into the security system. Run loops on the surveillance cameras. Unlock the electronic locks. Disarm the alarms. Can you do it?"

Corey looked uncertain. "I can try."

"No," Bones croaked in a voice that sounded a little like Kermit the Frog. "Try not. Do. Or do not. There is no try."

Maddock nodded to hide his surprise, which was as much at Bones' evident support of the plan as it was a response to the pop-culture reference. "Exactly. You've got this. We also need an extra pair of eyes to keep a lookout for security guards."

"You mean the drone?"

"I know it's a lot to juggle."

"I can help," Slava sounded almost as hesitant as Corey.

Maddock inclined his head to her. "Another pair of eyes won't hurt. I'll let Corey show you what he needs."

"When are we doing this?" asked Corey, his voice still brimming with anxiety.

Maddock checked his watch. It was just after nine in the evening. "How much time do you need for the hack?"

"Honestly, I have no idea."

"Then get started now. Bones and I have some

preparations of our own to make. We'll rendezvous at midnight."

10

Max Riddle was in denial, and he knew it. Try as he might, he just couldn't wrap his head around what had happened. He still half-expected Ashton Kutcher to jump out of the corner and yell "You just got punk'd, bitch!"

Or maybe Bones. That kind of seemed like his style.

But this prank had gone way past the point where it stopped being funny.

He had not suspected anything amiss as the young man in the dishwasher's apron led him through the kitchen and out the back door into a narrow alley behind the restaurant, and nobody else working there had given them a second look. Once out back, the young man pointed to a waiting van, and that started some alarm bells ringing, but against his better judgement he had allowed himself to be herded toward the van. The door had opened, revealing a man wearing a ski mask, and before Riddle could even think about crying out, a hand clamped over his mouth, pre-emptively silencing him.

Everything after that was a blur in his memory. He'd been tied up, gagged, and then someone had dropped a heavy sack over his head, which not only left him blind and mostly deaf, but barely able to breathe. He'd been forced to lay down, presumably on the floor of the van, and there he had stayed for what seemed like hours. He could tell the van was moving, but not much else. When it finally stopped, he was dragged out and placed in the chair where he now sat, still bound, gagged, and hooded.

Okay, guys, it's been funny, he wanted to say, *but now it's time for the reveal.*

As if in response to his unspoken thought, the hood was abruptly yanked off. The room in which he sat was dimly lit, but the light nevertheless stung his eyes which had grown accustomed to the total darkness. He blinked away tears, while greedily inhaling the cool air which, despite smelling of mildew, was relatively fresh. As the world gradually came into focus, he saw the man from the van, still wearing his ski mask, standing in front of him.

"I am going to remove the tape over your mouth," the man said in heavily accented English. "There is no one to hear you call for help, so you may as well save your breath. Do you understand?"

Riddle nodded, but then remembered that Bulgarians nodded to indicate 'no.' He shook his head instead, and then gave a helpless shrug.

The man uttered a short harsh sound that might have been a laugh, and then reached out and picked at a corner of the tape covering Riddle's mouth. With a quick tug, he ripped the adhesive away, taking what felt like a couple layers of skin with it.

"Ow," Riddle complained, but then looked up at the masked man, wondering what to say. If this was a prank, then the cameras were rolling and everything he said or did would be immortalized. But what response would play best? He could act tough—serious and unafraid—taking the situation at face value, the way Maddock might. That would go a long way toward establishing him as a rugged adventure hero, which might open all kinds of career opportunities. Or he could respond with snark, just like Bones probably would, showing the viewers that he was wise to the deception, too savvy to be so easily hoodwinked.

And if it wasn't a prank….

No, it has to be, he told himself.

The masked man regarded him silently for a few seconds, then spoke again. "Listen up. I don't want to kill you. Is bad for business. You don't give me any problems, and this will all be over soon."

The guy sounded pretty tough. Whomever was behind the prank, they were going for real authenticity. Riddle decided to split the difference—serious, but cocky. He rocked his head to one side then the other, hoping for an audible cracking of vertebrae—no such luck, but maybe they could add it in in post.

"What do you want?" he asked, and was pleased that there was not even the faintest quaver in his voice. "If you're after money, I'm afraid you've made a big mistake. I haven't got any, and if you were planning on going to my old network… Well, they'd probably pay you to not let me go."

The masked man chuckled. "Funny guy."

"Seriously. What do you want? How much do you actually think you can get for me?"

The man seemed to consider the question for a few seconds. "I suppose it doesn't hurt to tell you. I will trade you for the cup of Khan Krum."

"The cup?" Riddle could not hide his surprise. *What a twist,* he thought. *This is getting interesting.* "What do you want with it? Is this about the treasure map?"

The man stiffened. "Treasure map? What treasure map?"

Whoops. I guess he didn't know about that. Riddle tried dissembling. "Uh, the map that led us to the treasure."

"You're lying to me," the man said. The temperature in the room seemed to drop by several degrees. He moved in closer, bending down to look the seated Riddle directly in the eyes. Then, without any warning, his fist pistoned out and rammed into Riddle's unprotected solar plexus.

Riddle's breath was driven out in a gasp. The pain arrived an instant later as he was trying unsuccessfully to refill his lungs.

Okay, this definitely isn't cool anymore.

"Don't lie," the man said, his voice still as cold and hard as an iceberg.

Riddle's mouth hung open, but no sound came out and no air went in. Finally, the spasm passed and he was able to gasp in a breath. "This... Not... Prank...."

"What?" snapped the man. "Prank? You think this is some kind of joke."

Riddle swallowed. "No. Not a joke. A mistake. My mistake."

"Yes. Don't make another." The man put his hands on his hips. "Now, tell me about this treasure map."

11

It was exactly half an hour after midnight—zero-dark-thirty—when Maddock and Bones arrived in a quiet neighborhood about a quarter mile from the museum. Maddock pulled the Fiat to the curb and, after a quick look to make sure that no one was around to see them, they both got out. Maddock circled to the rear hatch, opened it, and took out the drone.

"Just hold it up," said Corey. "I'll take over from here."

Corey wasn't actually there with them. He and Slava were back at the hotel, manning the bank of computer hardware that would not only allow them to guide Maddock and Bones to their objective in real time, but also deal with all the electronic security measures that would stand in their way.

Maddock held the drone out at arm's length. "Ready when you are."

A few seconds later, the mini-aircraft's four rotor blades whirred noisily to life, and it leapt from his fingertips. As it rose higher, the buzz diminished to the point where it might easily be dismissed as insect noise or the hum of a power line.

Corey's disembodied voice issued from the bud in Maddock's right ear. "Okay, looking good. You're clear to move. There's a fence to the east—on your right. Climb it, and then head south along the fence line for about three hundred meters."

"Easy for him to say," Bones muttered, looking at the six-foot high metal barrier that stood in their way.

"At least there isn't any barbed wire," said Maddock.

Despite Bones' complaint, they easily vaulted the fence and began moving silently through the woods. Both men wore gray coveralls and leather work gloves, which they had "borrowed" from the hotel's maintenance office—not exactly the sort of high-speed 'tacti-cool' attire favored by cat-burglars in Hollywood blockbusters, but the best they could manage on short notice. They also had head-mounted GoPros, which were transmitting back to Corey via the same data relay that allowed for two-way comms and remote control of the drone. Bones carried a small backpack stuffed with an assortment of tools which, hopefully, they would not need. Maddock also had a backpack which was empty at the moment, though hopefully, it would not remain that way for long.

Corey guided them through a series of turns that kept them in the relative concealment of the trees until they emerged at the south end of the museum building. Several outdoor floodlights illuminated the open area in between, so they paused and waited for Corey to give them the go-ahead.

"Just sit tight for now," Corey advised. "If he stays on schedule, the night watchman will be in the conservation lab in about three minutes. After that, you should have at least thirty minutes to get in, grab, and go."

Maddock nodded absently. "Just say when."

No one had been more surprised than Corey at the ease with which he had cracked the museum's intranet, which had in turn given him full access to the security system—the alarms, all electronic doors, and the feed from the surveillance cameras located around and throughout the museum grounds. After a full two hours of watching the video, he was able to identify the roving night watchman's routine, and while there was nothing he could do to alter the guard's route, he could ensure that the man was in another part of the museum when Maddock and Bones made their move. He would also be able to loop the feed in those areas so that the two intruders would not appear on the monitor screens in the security office.

After about five minutes of waiting in silence, Corey gave the go ahead. Maddock and Bones stepped out from the woodline and started across the open area to an emergency exit located near the southwest corner. They moved with quick, confident steps, not running, but not creeping either. With Corey monitoring the area from multiple angles, including the hovering drone with its high-resolution camera, there was little chance of them happening upon someone, but in the event that they did, it would be much harder to pass themselves off as late night maintenance workers if they were skulking about like the thieves they were.

The precaution proved unnecessary. They reached the door and, right on cue, heard the click of the electronic lock disengaging. Maddock pulled the door open and stepped through, with Bones right behind him.

It took only a few minutes for them to make their way to the conservation lab, where Corey again opened the door to admit them. The lab was dark, so the two men produced MagLites equipped with red filters to navigate the maze of desks and workstations, to the table where they had last seen the cup of Khan Krum.

Maddock had been secretly hoping that the silver goblet would still be there, but the table had been cleared.

This was the part of the operation where things could go terribly wrong. It was a safe bet that the artifact was still there in the conservation lab, but to find it, they would have to conduct a thorough search—open every closet, cabinet and drawer—and that would take time. The longer they remained there—on the X, as they used to say back in their SEAL days—the more likely it was that someone would discover them.

"We should have brought Lady Luck along with us," Bones whispered as he shone a circle of red light on a placard with Cyrillic writing adorning a locked door. Maddock thought he was speaking figuratively, until Bones added. "I could use a translation."

Slava's voice came over the comms. "It's a warning that there are hazardous chemicals inside."

"So probably not the kind of place you'd store a priceless artifact."

"I wouldn't think so," she replied.

Maddock, on the other side of the room, had found plenty of towels, brushes, and other implements for cleaning and restoration, but no unsecured artifacts. "They must lock everything up at the end of the day," he ventured. "But if not in here, where?"

"Maddock," Bones whispered. "Over here. I think this is it."

Maddock left off his search and crossed the lab to join his friend. He was wondering why Bones had not asked Slava for another translation before making the determination, but when he got there, he saw why. There was no placard on the door before which Bones stood—just a sturdy looking metal handle and a round dial ringed with hashmarks and numbers in ten-digit intervals. It wasn't a closet; it was a vault.

"Well, crap."

Corey stared at the screen displaying the feed from Bones' GoPro and echoed the sentiment. He'd congratulated himself on being able to beat all the high-tech security measures, but he was helpless in the face of this low-tech mechanical barrier.

Bones however, just bent close to get a better look at the combination lock. "Maddock, hold the light for me,"

Maddock did as asked, while Bones stripped off his gloves, and then placed his left hand on the handle. The fingers of his right hovered above the dial. He rubbed his thumb and first two fingers together as if trying to warm them up, and then reached down and lightly touched the dial.

"Some of these old combos have what's called a 'day lock,'" he explained as he began rotating the dial slowly, testing the handle at each hashmark. "It's a short cut that lets you open the vault without having to dial the entire combination every time. It's useful if you have to open the door a lot during the day."

"But it's not daytime anymore," Corey countered.

"That doesn't matter," Bones replied, patiently. "All you have to do is find the last number of the combination, and it will open." After a few more attempts, he added with a sigh, "Unless the last person to close it spun the dial both ways to scramble it. Which is what it looks like happened here."

"Crap," Corey said again. "What do we do?"

Bones took his hands away from the dial and cracked his knuckles. "You just keep an eye on those cameras. This could take a while."

Corey realized that Bones was about to try beating the lock the old-fashioned way, listening for the clicks and feeling the subtle change in resistance that would signal the correct alignment of the internal mechanism. Corey had seen it done in movies, and knew that in real life, it wasn't nearly as simple as they made it look.

"There's got to be something we can do to help him,"

he muttered.

Slava, who had been watching at his elbow, offered a suggestion. "Do you see the name of the manufacturer there? Or a serial number? Maybe we can find the specifications of that particular door online. They might even have the combination on file."

Corey glanced over at her, suitably impressed and a little embarrassed that he hadn't thought of it first.

"No," Bones replied. "I looked. It's either been covered up or removed. Now be quiet and let me work."

Corey felt Slava's hand on his arm. "I have an idea," she whispered. "But you'll need to let me use the computer."

"Umm, I guess so, but what's your idea?"

"You hacked into the museum intranet, right? Maybe Dr. Ivanova sent or received the combination to the vault in an email, and forgot to delete it."

Corey considered this idea, and then nodded. "Yeah, that might work. Let me try a search of her emails."

"Do you read Bulgarian?" she countered.

That stopped him. "Uh, no. I can run it through a translation program."

"That will take too long, and the results will be unpredictable at best. I know how to do this. Allow me to, please."

Her confidence was as surprising to him as the urgency of her suggestion. "Uh, sure." He pushed a tablet with a Bluetooth-enabled keyboard toward her, and then returned his attention to the screen in front of him. "Okay, Bones. We're going to try something here."

Maddock's voice came back in a low whisper. "Bones is off comms for now. Keep me posted."

Corey didn't send a reply, but continued watching the different video feeds as the minutes ticked by. On the main screen, he saw Bones patiently turning the dial this way and that, occasionally trying the handle, but to no avail. The other screens showed mostly unchanging views of dimly lit hallways, exhibitions, and sidewalks, but once in a while, they revealed the watchman moving through with his flashlight to conduct a physical inspection.

Corey consulted the spreadsheet with the guard's schedule and then glanced at the time displayed in the corner of the screen. "Maddock, you've got about ten minutes until the guard comes through there again."

"Ten minutes isn't going to be enough time," Maddock replied. "Is there somewhere we can wait him out?"

"Maybe crawl under a table? He isn't very thorough."

"Crawl under a table," Maddock repeated, sounding dubious. "That's the best you can do?"

Before Corey could reply, Slava let out a cry of exultation. "I have it. She emailed the combination to one of her colleagues. It was still in her 'sent' file."

Corey keyed the toggle and relayed the news to Maddock, who in turn told Bones to get back on comms.

"Okay, genius," Bones said, "Let's have it."

Corey nodded to Slava who reeled off a string of two-digit numbers. She repeated them, but Bones was already spinning the dial, and before she finished, he gave the handle a turn.

"Open sesame," he said as the vault door swung open.

Corey pumped his fist in triumph. The view on the screen showed a first-person perspective of Bones stepping into the vault, which was the size of a large walk-in closet. The walls were lined with three levels of shelves, all of which were filled with various artifacts and objects.

Abruptly, the screen went dark, and then the words,

"Network connection lost—Try again?" appeared.

"Damn," he muttered, switching to Maddock's feed. "Dane, stay out of the vault."

But Maddock was already offline, too.

Corey glanced at the watchman schedule again. If Maddock and Bones weren't out of the conservation lab in six minutes, the guard would discover them. He checked the surveillance cameras again, scanning them quickly to locate the watchman, and his heart skipped a beat.

"Crap. He's running ahead of schedule."

"What?" Slava said, looking past him.

"He's rushing through. Maybe it's lunchtime or something. He's going to be there in a minute or two."

"Did you tell them?"

Corey shook his head. "I can't get a signal through the vault. There's too much interference." And even though he knew it would probably be futile, he tapped the "Try again?" prompt.

A little animated graphic of a spinning pinwheel appeared—the technical name for it was a "throbber"— indicating that the network was trying to re-establish contact. Several seconds passed and the wheel continued to spin.

On the other screen, the watchman ambled out of the view of one camera and into another, moving purposefully toward the door to the conservation lab.

"Come on, Maddock," Corey whispered. "Get the hell out of there."

As he entered the vault, Bones found the silver, skull cup resting on the middle shelf to his immediate right. He picked it up and turned to find Maddock right behind him, with his empty backpack held open to receive the artifact. As soon as it was nestled inside, Maddock zipped the bag closed, slung it over his shoulder, and headed out. Bones exited the vault after him, and as soon as he was out, he pushed the door shut, spun the dial, and then took a bandana from his pocket and wiped both dial and handle to remove any fingerprints.

"Corey," Maddock whispered. "How much time do we have?"

Bones looked up sharply. Something was wrong. Maddock's hoarse whisper should have been retransmitted through his earbuds after a millisecond of lag, but that had not happened.

"We're offline," he said. "The vault must have blocked the signal."

"Rookie mistake." Maddock shook his head in a display of chagrin. "I should have known better."

"Gasp. The infallible Pope Maddock makes a mistake? The apocalypse must be nigh."

Maddock ignored the comment. "Corey said we had about ten minutes, but I don't think we should move until we have him looking out for us."

Bones was about to signal his agreement when he heard a faint but familiar click come from the opposite side of the lab. Someone had just disengaged the electronic lock on the door.

"Crap," Bones whispered.

The two men looked at each other and then simultaneously said, "Table!" and then dropped flat and scurried under the nearest worktable as another barely audible click accompanied the turning of a doorknob.

Bones quickly switched off his red-hooded Maglite, at almost the same instant that a diffuse cone of white light swept the room right above his hiding space. He held his breath as the watchman entered the room, his shoes scraping softly on the carpeted floor.

A voice sounded in his ear, startling him. "Bones?" It was Corey. "Maddock? Are you receiving me? Hold your position."

No, really? Bones thought, but wisely kept his mouth shut.

The circle of light moving back and forth on the wall continued to shrink as the watchman moved closer.

Nothing to see here, jerkweed, Bones thought, as if he could somehow Jedi-mind trick the man.

As if in response, another voice broke the quiet—loud, unfamiliar, and speaking Bulgarian.

Crap. He knows we're here.

But there was something odd about the voice, and after a second or two, Bones realized that it wasn't the watchman, but rather a radio transmission on his walkie-talkie. The man replied in the same language, and then abruptly turned away, plunging the room into darkness once more as he hurried for the exit.

Bones decided to risk a question. "Corey, what the hell just happened?"

Corey's reply was uncertain. "Uh, I don't know if this is good news or bad, but something just tripped one of the alarms in the main hall. The guard is going to check it out."

"Does this have anything to do with us?" Maddock asked.

Slava answered the question. "I don't think so. The shift leader thinks it's just a malfunction." She paused a moment then added, "This might be a good time for you to get away."

"Corey is the coast clear?"

"It looks like it, but we'll have to be very careful about how we loop the video. Take it slow."

Bones and Maddock did just that, letting Corey talk them through every movement until they were outside the museum and once more moving through the trees surrounding the facility.

Ten minutes later, they were back in the Fiat, heading for the hotel, with Maddock once more at the wheel. Bones took the cup from the backpack and shone his red-hooded flashlight into the interior of the bowl, examining the inscription and the other markings and lines that might or might not have been mere natural deformities. The inspection revealed nothing that they had not already seen in the hi-def video footage.

"So what do you think?" he said. "Is this a treasure map?"

Maddock shook his head uncertainly. "Hard to say. Even if it is, we might be looking at this the wrong way. There was a fortune in gold coins in that cave where we found the cup. Maybe that's the treasure the inscription was talking about. Maybe somebody else followed the clues, found the treasure, and moved it there."

Bones grunted softly in acknowledgement. "But we're still going to check out that Eyes of God place, right?"

Maddock laughed. "Of course we are."

12

Six hours later, Maddock and Bones were back in the Fiat, heading east out of Sofia. Corey and Slava stayed behind, but would be providing real-time technical support via the same high-speed wireless data connection they had used the previous night. In the event that the police came calling, investigating their connection with the item that had been stolen from the museum, Slava would also, hopefully, be able to deflect suspicion and provide them all—including the absent Riddle—with an alibi. The possibility that they might be investigated was one reason that Maddock had decided to bring along the cup, which was still hidden away in his backpack. He also knew that it might contain clues that would only make sense once they reached their destination.

Maddock didn't really expect the search to bear fruit, but since they still had more than twelve hours before the kidnappers were supposed to make contact, it seemed prudent to check out Prohodna Cave before surrendering the cup, if only to cross the possibility off the list.

The drive took just over an hour and a half, much of it on a wide, four-lane divided highway that wended through forested hills. The skies remained overcast and on several occasions the windshield was spattered with drizzle. Four lanes eventually gave way to two, but traffic was light and they made good time. A wooden sign in the shape of a curving arrow, perched atop what looked like a stone chimney, signaled that they had arrived at their destination.

"Busy place," Bones remarked as they pulled off the

pavement onto a muddy track that curled south around the base of a low hill that they had just driven over. The track ended at a parking area which was crowded with tour vans.

"Slava said it was a popular destination," Maddock replied. He also recalled her saying that the cave's popularity made it an unlikely place to hide a treasure, but sometimes the best place to hide something was in plain sight.

After setting up their chest-mounted GoPros and establishing a data connection with Corey, they followed the rest of the arriving tourists down a path that disappeared into dense foliage. The trail descended as it skirted along the base of an overhanging limestone cliff which seemed to close in from both directions. Maddock surmised that they were at the bottom of what had, in prehistoric times, been an enormous sinkhole. When they rounded a corner and the arched opening came into view, Bones let out a low whistle. "That's a big ass hole."

Maddock gave him a sidelong glance. "Let's try to keep it family friendly, okay?"

Bones was not wrong about the size of the entrance, however. From bottom to top, it was at least a hundred feet.

"This is actually the small entrance to Prohodna," supplied Slava, still playing tour-guide, albeit remotely. "'Prohodna' means 'passage,' or literally, 'walkthrough.' The cave is a natural tunnel, almost three hundred meters long, through the hill. The large entrance is on the other end of the cave."

"We'll probably lose the signal once we go inside," Maddock said. "We'll do a slow sweep with the GoPros, and then upload the footage to you when we come out. Slava, is there anything else we absolutely need to know about this place?"

Slava seemed to ponder the question for a few seconds, then said, "An American movie was filmed here—one of the Expendables movies. I don't recall which one."

Bones snapped his fingers. "That's why it looks familiar. It was the one where Van Damme was the bad guy." He turned to Maddock. "Was that the second or third?"

Maddock shrugged. "I haven't seen them."

Bones rolled his eyes. "What, do they only show Hallmark Channel at the nursing home?"

"Come to think of it" Maddock continued, "I actually started watching one of them, but when Ronda Rousey showed up in that red dress, Angel made me turn it off."

"Ah," Bones said, nodding in understanding. "Gotcha."

Angel—Angela Bonebrake—was Bones' sister, and Maddock's ex-fiancé. She was also a successful mixed-martial arts fighter like Rousey had been.

The interior of the cave was no less awe-inspiring. There was no sense of claustrophobia here, not like in the manmade passage of the Tsarichina excavation. Instead, it was like being in a cathedral. After moving inside just a few steps, Maddock beheld the formation that had made the cave famous and inspired its alternate name. Directly overhead, the limestone ceiling was perforated by a pair of enormous holes—easily forty or fifty feet long—that were shaped exactly like eyes. Water trickled from the corners like tears, and streamed down the cave wall to collect in puddles on the floor. On a clear day, with the sun overhead, the eyes would probably have blazed with near-supernatural intensity.

Maddock and Bones moved slowly through the

immense chamber, inspecting every square inch of the cavern while their GoPros recorded everything for future perusal. While the domed ceiling overhead was relatively smooth and open, the floor was covered with sand and strewn with half-buried boulders, some larger than houses, forming a veritable maze through which they had to move slowly. To their left, a natural staircase, worn smooth in places by the feet of thousands of visitors, rose halfway up the wall, to a point almost directly beneath the hollow eyes. The wall to the right was mostly smooth, and upon it was a painted icon of a bearded figure that Maddock assumed represented Jesus. There were many small caves and recesses, but most were easily accessible and any treasure hidden within would have long ago been discovered and removed.

As he negotiated deeper into the maze of boulders, Maddock lost sight of both the entrance and the eyes, but he soon beheld the opening at the opposite end of the cave, what Slava had called "the large entrance," a scallop-like opening into the passage which rose well over a hundred feet above the craggy floor.

Suddenly, a scream pierced the stillness. Adrenaline jolted through Maddock, putting him instantly in "fight" mode. His stance widened, and every muscle in his body went tense, ready for action. He pivoted left, right, left again, seeking the source of the blood-curdling cry, which was growing louder with each passing millisecond, but the acoustics of the enormous cave made it impossible to pinpoint a location. From the corner of his eye, he saw Bones, similarly on alert, running to join him.

And then his eyes were drawn to movement outside the cave—a body falling like a meteor from somewhere above the entrance. Maddock quickly looked away to at least spare himself the sight of the terminal impact, and braced himself for the inevitable wet crunch.

But the expected splat did not happen. Instead, the protracted scream turned into something else—a cross between a whoop of elation and manic laughter.

Maddock risked a look and was astonished to see that the "body" had never quite reached the ground. In fact, it—or rather "she," for he could see clearly now that it was a young woman with a long brunette ponytail whipping around her head—was now "falling" up, rising back into the air like a yo-yo on a string. The simile was apt, for there was a string involved, or more precisely, a cord.

The rising figure vanished beyond the upper edge of the entrance, but then a moment later, fell once more into view, and now Maddock could clearly see the thick black belt around the woman's ankles, and the long yellow bungee cord to which it was attached.

"Friggin' thrill seekers," Bones muttered, shaking his head.

Maddock drew in a deep breath, willing his heart rate to return to normal. All he could think to say was, "Yeah."

Bones sighed and turned to face him. "See anything worth checking out in there?"

"A few possibilities. Let's get out in the open and upload to Corey. Maybe he'll see something we missed."

As they moved out from under the overhanging entrance to the cave, the woman, still hooting with glee at having survived her low-risk leap into the unknown, was being lowered slowly to the ground. A small crowd had gathered—fit-looking, college-aged men and women, attired in clingy Lycra outfits similar to what the bungee jumper was wearing.

"What do you know?" Bones remarked. "Must be a comic book convention nearby. That's some pretty lame cosplay, though."

"I was thinking Cirque Du Soleil," said Maddock.

Bones shook his head. "No, these guys look like nerds, not freaks. Not enough skin or goofy make-up."

What they looked like, at least to Maddock, was a group of adventure tourists, a supposition that was supported by the dozen or so mountain bikes parked nearby.

The young woman was unhooked from the bungee cord and helped to her feet, at which point the thick elastic cord began snaking back up the cliff to a spot high above the cave entrance. Several more people were gathered there, presumably waiting their turn. As Maddock stared up at them, an idea began to take shape.

"You know, maybe we need a different perspective," he said.

Bones gave him a sidelong glance. "What have you got in mind?"

"The inscription said to look for the treasure where God watches over you. Maybe we need to try looking at the cave through God's eyes. Up there."

Bones followed Maddock's gaze up to the crest overhead, and then nodded. "Not bad." He then turned and hiked over to join the Lycra-clad crowd. "Hola, chicas! Who can tell me how to get up there?"

The Lycra brigade turned out to be a group of German eco-tourists mountain-biking cross country from Sofia to Varna on the Black Sea coast—a journey of over four hundred miles, which would take more than two weeks, allowing for various diversions along the way. Bungee jumping from above the large entrance to the Eyes of God Cave was one such diversion.

One of the tourists, a buxom blonde named Ilsa, was

particularly helpful. After pointing them toward the trail leading up to the top of the cliff, she invited Bones and Maddock to follow her on Instagram.

As they made their way along the poorly maintained trail up to the top of the hill, where the remaining members of Ilsa's group were queued up and awaiting their turn to take the plunge, they were able to re-establish contact with Corey. Maddock quickly outlined their plan to get a top-down view of the cave.

"That's a good idea," Corey said. "If nothing else, it will give you something to do while the video is uploading. It will take a while to transfer everything."

"That's fine. Just tell us how to get to the eyes from here."

"Okay, let me look that up on Google Earth… It looks like they're due south of your position. About a hundred and twenty-five yards." He laughed, and added, "Don't fall in."

Corey's warning might have only been half-serious, but evidently the Bulgarian authorities were unconcerned about the risk. There were no barriers surrounding the formation—not even a guard rail. The terrain surrounding the twin almond-shaped holes was craggy and irregular, and dotted with sparse vegetation. The formation was at least a hundred feet across measured from the outer corners, which were conspicuously—and probably not coincidentally—oriented from east to west, but only about thirty feet wide. A natural bridge, just wide enough for a person to walk over, ran between the 'eyes.'

After a quick check to make sure that nobody was around to see them, Maddock and Bones approached the north edge of the western eye.

The view from above was surreal, but did not immediately reveal anything they had not seen from below. Both men stared down into the depths of the cavern for several seconds before Bones broke the silence. "You see anything?"

"No. I've got an idea, though."

Maddock scooted back from the edge, unslung his backpack, and after another quick look around to ensure privacy, removed the cup. He rotated it so that the eye sockets of the skull were aligned with the twin holes, and then peered over them at the inscription and the odd pattern of lines in the bowl. After committing it to memory, he returned his gaze to the opening and began looking for anything on the cavern floor that remotely resembled the interior of the cup. After nearly two full minutes of looking, he got up and moved down to the east eye. When the change in perspective yielded no better results, he crossed the bridge and tried again from the southern side of each eye.

Finally, he shook his head. "Nothing. Either we're misinterpreting the inscription and the treasure is somewhere else, or—"

"Or there is no treasure," Bones finished.

Maddock nodded. "Aside from what we found at Tsarichina." He rocked back on his haunches and sighed in disappointment. "Well, I guess it was always a longshot. Maybe we should just focus on getting Max back safely."

He was returning the cup to his pack when Bones hissed an urgent warning. "We've got company."

Fearing that someone was coming to investigate them, Maddock hastily zipped the pack shut and slung it over one shoulder. As he did, two men stepped out of the woods to the north.

His initial concern that the men might be park rangers or police officers coming to scold them for trespassing was allayed when he saw that the men were wearing ordinary street clothes, but his relief was short-lived. The two men didn't look like wide-eyed tourists. Both were light-skinned and stocky. One looked to be in his mid-twenties, and wore blue jeans and a red T-shirt that showed off muscular, tattooed arms. The other might have been his older brother. He wore a Navy-blue polo shirt, open at the throat to reveal a gold chain and cross pendant, and khaki slacks.

Maddock's first thought was that they looked like wanna-be gangsters. Tough guys.

His second thought was, *Uh, oh.*

13

As soon as eye contact was made, the two men abandoned any semblance of subtlety. The younger man dug into a pocket and produced a butterfly knife, which he opened with a theatrical flourish. "Hand over cup," he said, "And nobody will get hurt."

Maddock retreated until he was standing just a few steps from the eyes. Bones however, stood his ground. "Looks like somebody hasn't heard the old saying about bringing a knife to a gunfight."

Maddock shot him an incredulous look, but Bones just nodded. "You know… The gun you brought along? In your backpack?"

Maddock finally got it. "Oh, that gun." He jammed his hand deep into the backpack, curling his fingers around the stem of the cup, and then without drawing it out, pointed it—pack and all—at the man with the knife. "That's close enough."

The man balked, clearly not willing to call Maddock's bluff, but his partner just laughed. "Is no problem," he said, and then reached down and raised the hem of his polo shirt to reveal a revolver stuffed into his waistband, right above his fly. He drew the gun and brandished it. "I bring gun to gunfight. But I don't think *you* did." He jabbed the weapon at Maddock emphatically.

Bones shrugged. "Well, it was worth a shot."

"Plan B," Maddock murmured, barely loud enough for Bones to hear, and then extended the hand holding the backpack out to the side, conspicuously positioned over the edge of the hole. "You got me. Come and get it."

The man visibly recoiled in alarm as the implicit threat sank in, which was exactly what Maddock had been hoping for. As the gun barrel dipped, Maddock spun on his heel and darted across the narrow bridge, then took off running, angling around the perimeter of the eyes toward the southwest. Bones, correctly interpreting Maddock's message—in such situations, and without an established contingency, "plan B" was code for improvise, adapt, or simply run like hell—followed in Maddock's footsteps to the opposite side of the eyes, but turned toward the southeast. This had the desired effect of dividing the gunman's attention, hopefully buying them a few critical seconds to get out of range and find concealment in the woods.

But in the instant that Maddock turned away, he realized that the two *mutri* thugs were not alone. During the brief standoff, four more mobsters had approached from the south, guns drawn, to block Maddock's intended escape route.

He immediately pivoted heading northwest to skirt around the formation, and saw the man with the revolver moving to cut him off. The fact that he had not fired his weapon seemed like a positive sign to Maddock, but there was no telling how long the mobster would continue to exercise restraint, so instead of trying to evade the man, Maddock adjusted course and charged toward the man like a guided missile.

The mobster's eyes widened in surprise and fear as Maddock bore down on him. He tried to bring his gun up, but before he could take aim, Maddock plowed into him, bowling him off his feet. Maddock didn't wait around to see how long it would take the man to recover, but kept going, sprinting toward the woods.

Harsh shouts followed him, but then a different voice

intruded—Corey's. "Dane, what's going on there?"

"Can't talk now," Maddock rasped, not slowing, but then realized that his friend might be able to offer some help. "Is Bones all right?"

"He's running through the woods like you," Corey responded. "That's about all I can tell you."

A moment later, Bones' voice, slightly breathless, came over the line. "I managed to draw a couple of them off," he said. "But I think they know you've got the cup."

"*Who* knows?" Corey asked. "Who's chasing you?"

Before either Maddock or Bones could answer, Slava spoke up. "*Mutri.*" She spat the word like a curse. "They followed you from Sofia. Don't go back to your car. They'll probably try to ambush you there."

That seemed like sound advice to Maddock, but it wasn't a solution to his immediate problem. "Well then, where should we—"

The question was left unfinished as Maddock abruptly broke through the trees and found himself facing another group of people—not Bulgarian mafiosi, but Lycra-clad eco-tourists. One of them, a young woman, had a thick, padded shackle around her ankles, and attached to it was a long yellow cord that disappeared into a serpentine coil.

He angled to their left to avoid a collision. It was a reflex action, but even as he shifted course, the significance of what he had just beheld sank in. Then he saw the precipice before him and the emptiness beyond.

He arrested his stride, but his momentum carried him forward, skidding toward the drop. Hoping a fall onto his backside might save him from a fatal plunge, he threw his arms wide and arched backward. Whether the desperate maneuver would have worked became irrelevant as one of the men standing at the edge caught hold of his outflung hand and hauled him back. The abruptness of the move caused them both to lose their balance. They landed in a tangle of limbs behind the other two.

Maddock was grateful for the assist but there wasn't time to thank the man. Squirming out from under his rescuer, he bounded to his feet and looked around until he spied the trail leading back down to the bottom of the drop off and the large entrance to the cave. But before he could start toward it, two of the mobsters erupted from the foliage, waving pistols and looking for someone to shoot. One of them was between Maddock and the trailhead.

Maddock considered trying to bulldoze past the man, but immediately rejected the idea. If it had been just him against the gunman, he might have risked it, but the presence of three innocent bystanders changed that calculation. In a flash of inspiration, he realized there was a way to take himself and one of those bystanders out of the equation.

As the gunman took aim, Maddock slung the backpack over one shoulder, and turned to the female adventure tourist standing on the edge of the precipice. "Sorry," he said, and then without any further explanation, pushed her out into nothingness.

Even as the woman disappeared from view, Maddock snatched up a loop of the bungee cord that was snaking out after her, and then leapt from the precipice as well.

As gravity caught hold of him, he whipped his body around the cord, hooking his right ankle around it. He was only a few feet above the woman, but because the cord was attacked to her ankles and she had already turned upside-down, he couldn't see her face, but he could hear her screaming.

Maddock had never bungee jumped before, but between multiple parachute jumps in the SEALs and years of rock climbing, he had plenty of experience with long falls and a good sense of what was about to happen. His training and experience did not entirely nullify the instinctive adrenaline rush that accompanied a high jump, but it did allow him to think clearly and utilize the very brief interval of the fall to improve his position and plan for the next step of his insane escape plan.

When the slack—probably a good fifty feet of it—was gone, the elastic cord began to both stretch and tighten around Maddock's body. Simultaneously, the rate at which he was falling began to diminish, though not nearly as much as with a parachute opening or a climbing fall. In the latter instance, the dynamic rope used for belay lines only stretched about twenty or thirty percent, which caused a noticeable, though not usually injurious jolt. Judging by what he'd seen during the jumps he and Bones had witnessed, he guessed the bungee cords had at least a hundred percent elasticity—doubling in length under the weight of an average person. He probably wouldn't even start to feel resistance until it reached fifty percent of its unstretched length. The one thing he could not even begin to estimate was how far the cord would stretch under the weight of two people.

The cord grew tighter around his waist and leg, like a python just starting to squeeze the life out of him. The ground was rushing up faster than he would have liked, but he could tell that the resistance from the bungee was increasing, slowing his rate of descent, though not nearly enough. The addition of his weight to that of the young woman actually attached to the cord had increased the stretch-length beyond the distance separating the top of the cave entrance from the ground below, which in practical terms meant that she would plow headfirst into the rocks—an unquestionably fatal impact—and a fraction of a second later, he would hit feet first—potentially survivable, but not without serious injuries.

Neither outcome was acceptable to Maddock.

He quickly unhooked his foot from around the cord, and then thrust himself away from it, surrendering entirely to a free fall.

The bungee cord immediately went taut, completely arresting the woman's descent. Maddock thought he heard the pitch of her scream change a little, and worried that his stunt might have injured her, but there was nothing to be done about it now. She flashed past him, shooting back up into the air at the end of the cord while he completed his descent without any restraint whatsoever.

It was only about twenty feet to the ground—the equivalent of stepping off the roof of a two-story building—but because he had already been falling, albeit at a greatly reduced rate, the impact was brutal. He knew to pitch himself sideways at the instant his feet made contact, utilizing a technique known as a parachute landing fall, which helped to distribute some of the shock, but it still hurt like hell. A lightning bolt of pain shot up from the soles of his feet to his lower back, followed almost right away by a series of hammer-like blows as the rest of his body made contact with the uneven rock terrain just outside the cave entrance.

He was still alive, but for a few seconds, that was the only thing of which he was certain. The initial pain accompanying the shock receded, but only a little. He felt like he'd been stabbed bone deep and all over with electrically charged blades.

But he knew he had to get moving. It would only take the mobsters a few minutes—five at most—to descend the trail. He needed to be long gone when they arrived.

With a near-superhuman effort, he rolled over onto

his stomach and then managed to push up onto hands and knees. He still hurt all over, and while none of it felt like the pain he associated with broken bones, when he tried to stand up, a stabbing sensation shot up from his left ankle. It bore his weight, but running on it would be impossible. The best he could hope for was a fast hobble, and that wouldn't keep him ahead of the mobsters for long.

Ilsa and some of the other adventure tourists approached cautiously to see if he was all right, but he brushed aside their inquiries, looking past them until he spied a better means of escape.

Gritting his teeth against the pain, he pushed through the group and limped over to where their mountain bikes were parked in two orderly rows. The bicycles were all the same color, with shock absorbers on the front forks, but those were the only common features they shared. About half of them featured the drop tube design for female riders, and there was a range of frame sizes. They weren't locked up, but one Lycra-clad rider appeared to be guarding them. He watched Maddock approach with a raised eyebrow and a bemused expression.

Despite his grimace of pain, Maddock did his best to affect a look of nonchalance as he walked in front of the bikes. When he arrived at one that looked to be about the right size, he looked over at the man and asked, "Is it okay if I borrow this?"

The man shook his head, clearly not comprehending the question.

Before Maddock could even attempt an explanation, a disturbance from the direction of the trail leading back to the top seized the man's attention. Maddock looked too, just as the young, tattooed *mutri* thug blundered out of the vegetation, searching for his escaped quarry. The man was flushed and breathing heavily from the exertion, but his carriage remained erect, poised for action.

With the attendant and everyone else fixated on the man with the knife, Maddock saw his opportunity. He grabbed the handlebars, pulled the bike toward him, then sidestepped, and swung his leg over the bike's top post, settling onto the seat. He got his left foot on the corresponding pedal, and pushed off with his other foot, propelling the bike forward.

A harsh shout chased after him, though whether it was the mobster or one of the tourists realizing the bike had been stolen, Maddock couldn't say, and he had no intention of looking back to check. He found the right pedal with his foot, and pedaled furiously away from the cave entrance.

His ankle throbbed a little when he pressed down, but it was far less painful than walking. In a matter of just a few seconds, he reached the trail leading into the woods. Once he was somewhat concealed by the trees, he twisted the gear selector on the left handgrip, which caused the front derailleur to push the chain over onto the smallest chain ring. As he expected, the amount of resistance from the pedals diminished almost to nothing, and he had to pedal furiously just to keep moving forward, but this allowed him to ride up the incline without expending a lot of energy or aggravating his ankle injury. The ascent was mercifully short. He soon emerged from the woods onto a flank of the hill that covered the Eyes of God cave. He guessed that riding up the hill would bring him to the highway and eventually to the parking lot, but that was the first place the mobsters would probably think to look for him. They might even be lying in ambush.

It was time to ask for a little guidance. "Corey, help me out here," he shouted.

When there was no immediate answer, he called out

again. "Corey, I need a direction. Are you still with me?"

Once again, the only response was silence. It occurred to him that he might have lost his earbud, but a quick check confirmed that it was still plugged into his ear canal. Reluctantly, he applied the brakes, and when he was fully stopped, reached into his pocket for his phone. As soon as his fingers made contact with it, he could feel that something was wrong with the device. Evidently, it had been caught between him and one of the rocks in the landing zone following his improvised bungee leap. Despite being nestled inside a protective OtterBox case, his phone now had a nearly forty-five-degree bend in the middle.

"Well, crap," he muttered, shoving the useless phone back into his pocket.

Without Corey to guide him, he would have to simply pick a direction and hope for the best. He pointed the bike downhill and shoved off, letting gravity do most of the work. In seconds, he was flying down the slope.

The hillside was dotted with trees and shrubs, and the terrain was rocky and uneven, but the bike was designed for just such conditions. As he whipped the handlebars back and forth, slaloming through the trees, Maddock resisted the impulse to ride the brakes. Instead, he shifted his weight backward, with his arms fully extended, until his backside was off the seat and hanging just a few inches above the rear tire. This lowered his center of gravity so that, in the event of an abrupt stop, he would not be catapulted over the handlebars. That was a good thing since he was picking up speed and the landscape ahead was a veritable minefield of rocks, holes, and tree roots. Some were big enough to require a course correction, but most could be taken head on, provided he lifted up on the handlebars popping a modified wheelie in the instant before contact. Rather than fixate on every obstacle in his path, he instead tried to keep his focus on the ever-changing spot about fifteen to twenty feet directly ahead, which gave him just enough time to decide whether to go over or around each hazard.

Unfortunately, it also meant that he didn't see that the slope ended in an abrupt drop-off, until it was too late to stop.

14

After separating from Maddock, Bones had initially chosen stealth over speed, staying low and seeking concealment in the foliage near the twin holes which looked down into Prohodna cave, but when it became apparent that most of the men were pursuing Maddock, Bones decided to change tactics. He rose from hiding and began crashing noisily through the woods, hoping to draw at least some of the men after him. He was only partly successful. Two of the Bulgarian mobsters split off from the larger pack and came after him.

The men clearly had no experience with tracking prey through the woods. They blundered through the vegetation, shouted to each other, and seemed unable to pick up the very obvious trail Bones was leaving.

When reporting his progress to Corey, Bones didn't even make an effort to whisper. He was dismayed however when Slava warned against returning to the car. How else were they supposed to get back to civilization?

Maddock started to ask exactly that question, but was cut off in mid-sentence. The sound of a scuffle ensued, followed a few seconds later by a scream that was audible even without the amplification of the two-way communications link. After a second or two however, the random noise coming through the earpiece ceased completely.

Bones' felt a flush of apprehension—something terrible had just happened.

"Crap!" Corey said, his tone urgent and anxious.

"What's wrong?" Bones snapped.

Corey spoke slowly, like someone half-asleep and trying to make sense of a bad dream. "Uh, Dane just pushed a woman off a cliff. He jumped after her, and then his feed went black. I think…" He trailed off, as if fearful that voicing the obvious conclusion might make it a reality.

Bones broke from concealment and charged back toward the trail that had brought them to the hilltop. This time, he made no noise whatsoever, and when he spoke again, it was barely a whisper. "What do you mean, 'jumped after her'? Like bungee jumped?"

"Maybe." Corey didn't sound particularly hopeful. "But that wouldn't explain why I lost the feed."

Bones spied movement about thirty yards ahead—one of the mobsters, emerging from behind a thicket—and shifted course to give the man a wide berth. "Could he have ducked back into the cave?"

"Maybe," Corey said again, with the same note of skepticism.

Bones shook his head. There was only one way to know for certain what had happened. Throwing caution to the wind, he broke into a full sprint, choosing the most direct course back to the clifftop above the large entrance, which took him right past the *mutri* thug. The man's head swiveled around as he detected movement, but before he could process what he was seeing, Bones plowed into him and sent him sprawling. Bones didn't slow down and he didn't look back.

He emerged from the woods only a few steps away from the bungee staging area, and saw a several people, presumably members of the adventure tour group, standing near the edge, cautiously looking down. Steeling himself against the grimmest possible outcome, Bones stepped up beside them and gazed down as well.

A hundred fifty feet below, a few members of the group were helping a young thrill-seeker detach from an ankle harness. The rest of the group was gathered near the mountain bikes and appeared to be arguing about something.

There was no sign of Maddock, nor did it appear than anyone had jumped or fallen from the cliff, aside from the young woman attached to the bungee cord.

Frowning, Bones turned to the adventure-tourist beside him. "What's going on?" he asked, trying to sound casual.

Without looking at him, the man replied, "Some madman pushed Marta before she was ready. Then he grabbed her cord and tried to go down with her."

Bones allowed himself a faint sigh of relief. That was a detail Corey had not picked up on. "Wow. Did it work?"

"He almost got himself killed," the man replied. Bones thought he sounded pretty pissed off, but with the German accent, it was hard to tell. "And Marta, too."

"But she's okay," Bones pointed out. "So what happened to the guy?"

"He landed hard, but got up and ran off. Some men were chasing him." The man paused a beat, and then snarled contemptuously. "I think he must have been a thief. He stole one of our bikes."

Definitely pissed off, Bones thought, hiding a smile at the thought of Maddock committing grand theft bicycle. "Bummer," he said. "Well, I hope you get it back."

"*Danke,*" the man said, and then finally turned to look at Bones. His eyes immediately went wide. "Wait. You were with him. With the madman."

Bones affected a look of innocent outrage. "No way, dude. I don't hang out with madmen. Except for my uncle, Crazy Charlie, and the craziest thing he ever did was buy a casino in Canada."

The man shook his head. "No, I remember. You came up with him."

Bones was already backing away, but at that moment, one of the *mutri* men burst out of the trees. He took that as a cue to accelerate his exit.

As he charged down the trail leading back to the entrance, he said, "Did you get that?"

"Yeah," Corey replied, sounding as relieved as Bones felt. "He must have smashed his phone when he landed." He paused a beat, then added, "How are we going to regain contact with him?"

"Don't worry about Maddock," Bones said. "He'll call in as soon as he can. He knows what he's doing."

At that precise moment, Maddock would not have shared Bones' confidence in his ability to deal with the situation.

The downhill slope had, without warning, terminated at a sharp drop-off. Beyond that stark horizontal line, there was only the indistinct green of a distant forest. A fraction of a second, which brought him that much closer to the edge, revealed another band of color—the gray-green of a river flowing perpendicular to the slope, and directly below the cliff.

Maddock felt an almost primal urge to squeeze the brakes, or throw himself off the bike to avoid going over, but knew such a course of action would not only prove futile, but possibly make matters worse. Instead, he used what little time remained to spin the pedals even faster, supplying a boost of speed as the mountain bike's tires left the ground, and both bike and rider arced out into the air above the water.

The fall was only about thirty feet, and unlike the

drop from the bungee cord, ended with a plunge into the far more yielding surface of the river. Maddock's last-second decision to pedal furiously supplied just enough momentum to carry him out into the slightly deeper water away from the sheer walls of the gorge. Nevertheless, he had been falling fast enough that, even as the water closed over his head, he felt the bike's impact with the river bottom travel up through the pedals to his feet, eliciting a slight jolt of pain in his injured ankle.

Instinctively, he kicked away from the bike and, with one hand gripping the strap of the duffel bag containing the skull cup, began kicking back for the surface. He could feel that the current had him, but he didn't fight it. Once his head was clear of the water, he simply allowed the river to carry him along.

The western shore, to his left, was thickly forested and looked accessible, provided he could reach it. Whether or not anything remotely resembling civilization lay beyond those woods, he could not say. To his right, there was only a sheer rock wall which continued to rise higher and higher as he was swept along, but at its crest stood a large multi-story structure which appeared to have been at least partly built into the cliff wall. It looked like it might be a resort hotel. As he was pondering what it might take to reach it, another man-made object came into view. A hundred yards directly ahead, a low bridge spanned the river, disappearing into the woods on either side. He let the river carry him past the tall cylindrical piers supporting the bridge arches. Just beyond it, the river veered away from the cliff. A low forested bank appeared in front of Maddock and he swam toward it, pulling himself up onto dry ground.

Maddock wanted nothing more than to lie there and rest, but knew that he had to keep moving, so he got to his feet and limped up the gentle slope toward the bridge and the adjoining road. After a few steps, his ankle actually felt a little better, which told him that the injury wasn't as severe as he had earlier feared. He wouldn't be running any marathons anytime soon, but he would be able to hobble along for at least a few miles.

He was a little dismayed to discover that the road was actually a railroad, and that it continued north along the base of the cliff. Railroads, Maddock knew, sometimes crossed hundreds of miles of open country without encountering cities or even minor settlements. He didn't recall having crossed any train tracks during the drive to Prohodna, which meant that following the rails back across the bridge would not bring him to the highway. There was no guarantee that following the tracks north would get him anywhere he wanted to go, but staying on the same side of the river made the most sense, so he stepped onto the rail bed and started walking.

His choice proved fortunate. As he walked along, the cliff to his right began sloping down until, after only about a tenth of a mile, it was nothing more than a grassy hillside running parallel to the rails. Rather than tempt fate by continuing on into the unknown, Maddock instead ventured up the hill and headed back up the slope along the rising crest. Near the top, he was forced to free climb a few sections, but eventually reached the structure he had glimpsed earlier.

The building was perched on the edge of the cliff. Approaching it from the road to the east, it would have looked like a large two-story house, but Maddock's view from the river revealed its true size. There was a sign on the gabled second story, but Maddock couldn't decipher the Cyrillic writing. Not for the first time since his ill-advised bungee-plummet, he regretted the loss of his phone. Slava could have told him exactly where he was. Nevertheless, the sign suggested a place of business rather than a private residence. The A-frame chalkboard sign on the porch, adorned with a Bulgarian beer logo that he recognized, seemed to confirm this deduction.

He ventured inside, and soon found himself in what appeared to be an empty restaurant dining room. A young man standing behind the bar, polishing glasses, raised his head and seemed about ready to call out a greeting, but when he beheld Maddock, his eyes went wide in alarm.

Maddock grimaced, realizing that he must look like an escaped madman. His clothes were still damp and the long trek up the cliff had left him streaked with dirt and grime. He quickly raised his hands in a placating gesture and said, "Sorry, I'm really, really lost. Can you help me?"

The man's wary expression immediately softened, and he broke into a grin. "You are American?" he asked in halting English.

"That's right. I was visiting Prohodna and got lost. Then I sort of fell into the river."

The man's eyebrows arched in surprise. "You fell in Iskar River?"

"Yeah. It's a long story. The thing is, my phone got ruined. Can I make a call…" He noticed a large computer monitor at one end of the bar. "Or better yet, would you mind if I check my email?"

15

Boyan Dragomirov stood at the precipice above the large entrance to Prohodna cave, staring down at the commotion below. Although he couldn't make out what was being said, it wasn't hard to figure out.

When his younger brother, Krasimir, had attempted to catch up to Maddock on his stolen bicycle, the crowd had decided to make Krasimir the target of their ire, blaming him for the theft. Rather than ignoring the baseless accusations and simply walking away, Krasimir had rashly decided to respond in kind, posturing and threatening his accusers, escalating the already tense situation.

Dragomirov sighed and turned to one of his lieutenants. "Nikolay. Go drag him out of there before he kills someone."

The man shook his head, but before departing to carry out the order, asked, "What about Maddock?"

"We'll find him. Besides, we still have something he wants." Almost as the words were uttered, Dragomirov felt his phone vibrating in his pocket.

He took it out, looked at the name displayed on the screen, and frowned. It read "Krasimir," but obviously, his brother was not the one making the call. He thumbed the virtual button to accept the call and held it to his ear. "Atanas. Why are you calling? I'm busy."

"I'm aware," came the reply. The electronic voice modulator did not transmit sarcasm very well, but Dragomirov nevertheless picked up on it. "What in God's name do you think you're doing? This was never the plan."

"I made a new plan," Dragomirov replied. "You did not tell me the cup has a map to the treasure of Tsar Samuil."

"I did not know. But it doesn't matter. You would have been free to go after the treasure as soon as Maddock gave you the cup."

Dragomirov uttered a harsh laugh. "Do you think I'm an idiot? Why do you think Maddock came to Prohodna? He was trying to find the treasure."

"There is no treasure at Prohodna," said Atanas.

Dragomirov mulled this response for a moment. "How do you know?"

"It doesn't matter. All that matters is that you back off. Maddock will give you the cup in exchange for Max Riddle, as planned. Then you can do whatever you like."

Dragomirov nodded. "I don't think I like your plan anymore. I have a better one. And I don't need you anymore."

"Is that what you think? Do not cross me. You don't want someone like me for an enemy."

"Are you actually threatening me?" Dragomirov laughed again, this time with real humor. "You've got balls, computer man. I respect that. But don't push it, or you'll find out what it means to have *me* for an enemy."

He took the phone away, cutting short any further protest, and thumbed the button to end the call. Atanas might do something foolhardy, like contacting the police, but even if he did, Dragomirov wasn't that worried. He had friends in high places who owed him favors.

The phone rang again almost immediately, but Dragomirov ignored it. *I must tell Krasimir to get a new phone,* he thought to himself, and then put the device in his pocket. In the same motion, he withdrew another phone—the one he had taken from Riddle. He had turned it off after the abduction, fearing that it might be used to trace his location. Atanas had handled the ransom call using a cloned version of the phone, and had assured Dragomirov that the phone was untraceable, but now that he could no longer count the hacker as an ally, he would have to proceed very carefully.

He opened it to the contacts list and found the number for the woman from the ministry of tourism. She picked up on the first ring, and said in a cautious voice, "Hello?"

"You know who this is?"

There was a long pause. "You kidnapped Max."

"That's right. There is new plan. Tell Dane Maddock that if he wants to see his friend again, he will need to give me more than just the cup of Khan Krum. I want the treasure of Tsar Samuil."

Another pause, and then, "You promised to exchange Max for the cup."

"I know I did. But I changed my mind."

"We don't even know if the treasure is real."

"That is your problem. If you want your friend back, you had better find it. I give you three days. Call me at this number when you have it, not before." He hung up without waiting for a reply, and then turned his attention to the situation on the ground below. Nikolay had succeeded in tearing Krasimir away from the angry tourists.

Good, he thought. *Now to pick up Maddock's trail again.*

When Dane Maddock finally discovered the treasure, Dragomirov would be right behind him. He had no doubt that there was a treasure, or that Maddock and his friends would succeed in finding it, but he had no intention of exchanging it for Max Riddle's life. Once the treasure was in his possession, he would kill them all.

The barkeeper apologized for his initial reaction. Apparently, he actually had thought Maddock was an escaped mental patient—from the Bulgarian State Psychiatric Hospital which was located on the opposite side of the river.

The building perched on the clifftop, he went on to explain, was the National Cave House, sometimes called the Peter Tranteev House, in honor of the founder of the Bulgarian Speleological Society. It was primarily an educational institution, though it also served as both a restaurant and a hostel serving visitors to Prohodna and the dozens of smaller caves in the surrounding area. Maddock was a little worried that Ilsa and the rest of the Lycra-clad eco-tourists might show up at any minute, or worse, that the *mutri* thugs might think to look for him there, so he quickly began composing an email to Corey. But as he started explaining what he needed his friend to do in order to get him back to Sofia, he reconsidered that course of action.

It occurred to him that the *mutri* had done a particularly good job of tracking their movements. They had learned of the discovery at Tsarichina mere hours after the cup of Khan Krum was handed over to the museum. They had known exactly where to find Max, and executed the abduction from the restaurant too perfectly for it to have been a spur of the moment action. And while he had not exactly been diligent about checking for a tail during the long drive to Prohodna, Maddock felt sure he would have noticed someone following them. All of which told him that the *mutri* had some other method of keeping tabs on them, and until he had a better idea of what that was, he couldn't risk contacting the others.

But there was one person outside that small group who might be able to help.

Closing the email program, he instead opened an IRC chat client and sent a direct message to his friend Jimmy Letson.

Maddock had met Jimmy in the Navy during the first phase of SEAL training. They had quickly become friends, and even though Jimmy had washed out during Hell Week, they had stayed in touch over the years. After leaving the Navy, Jimmy had become an investigative reporter for the *Washington Post*, but his true talent was research, particularly in the digital realm. Though he disdained the term, Jimmy was a master hacker.

The chat client chimed as Jimmy's response appeared. "Yo, Maddock. How did you know my liquor cabinet was nearly empty?"

Jimmy often helped Maddock with research into esoteric topics relating to their treasure hunts, always taking payment in the form of distilled spirits, usually Wild Turkey bourbon.

Maddock grinned and typed, "As much as I feel I should encourage you to give your liver a break, I really need some help."

"You let me worry about my liver," Jimmy replied. "What can I do you for?"

Maddock quickly summarized the events of the past two days, concluding with his suspicion that the Bulgarian mafia might be conducting electronic surveillance on one or all of them.

"You're right to be concerned about that," Jimmy said. "Bulgaria is home to some of the craftiest black hats I've ever run across. Some of them are absolute legends in the community."

"So can you tell if someone has hacked us?"

"Sure. If I had to guess, I'd say someone probably cloned your phones. I'll do a location check and see if there are duplicates." There was a brief pause and then, "I'm only pinging one phone for you. Are you in Sofia?"

Maddock frowned, feeling a growing sense of dread. "No, I'm about a hundred miles north of there. But my phone was smashed."

"Sorry to be the bearer of bad news, but you've been cloned. I'll check Bones' phone as well. Who else do I need to look at?"

"Corey." He typed in the digits for Corey's cell from memory. "And you should probably check Slava's number, too. I don't have it, but I'm sure you can find it. Slava Kostadinova. She works for the Ministry of Tourism."

This time, the pause was much longer, but when the chat screen finally flashed with Jimmy's paragraph-long reply, Maddock's sense of dread blossomed into something approaching full-blown nausea.

"Holy crap," he murmured.

As SEALs, Bones and Maddock had received extensive training in SERE—survival, escape, resistance, and evasion—which in practical terms meant that, if they had to, they could make their way, undetected, through hostile territory.

Fortunately for Bones, he did not need to call upon these skills in order to get back to Sofia. Instead, Corey had found a ride-share driver who was more than willing to convey Bones to that destination in relative comfort. Bones spent the next ninety minutes stretched out in the back seat of the car, working on the immediate problem of how to get Riddle back without either the cup of Khan Krum or the treasure, which might not even exist.

He did not go straight to the hotel, but instead had his driver drop him off a few blocks away, near the statue of Sveta Sofia. He chose the place, not because of a desire to get a better look at the provocative monument, but rather because it was a reference point he could use to make the remainder of the journey on foot, all the while checking to make sure nobody was following him. The surveillance detection route added an additional forty-five minutes to the journey, but by the time he entered the hotel, he was reasonably certain that the *mutri* were not following him.

He found Corey and Slava sitting at a table in the casino lounge—a public place where, hopefully, the mobsters would not dare make a move against them.

"Any luck tracing Max's phone?" he asked, eschewing preamble as he joined them.

"Actually, yes," Corey replied. "Last time I checked, it was in Prohodna,"

"Of course it was." Bones sighed. "So it's with the mobsters. I doubt they brought Max with them."

"We could always go to the police."

"I don't think that's a good idea," Slava broke in. "*Mutri* have informants in the police and government. Even if you found someone trustworthy, the kidnappers would find out."

"I agree," Bones said. "We go to the authorities only as a last resort."

"So what does that leave us?" Corey asked.

"These mobsters want a treasure," said Bones. "Let's give them one."

"We don't even know if there is a treasure," Corey

protested. "We tried telling them that."

"What about the gold coins we found at the bottom of the Tsarichina Hole. Those have got to be worth something."

"Oh, yeah," Corey said, slowly. "I forgot about that."

Slava pointed out the obvious flaws in Bones' strategy. "Max may have already told the kidnappers about the treasure at Tsarichina. For all we know, they already have it."

Bones scratched his chin. "Yeah, that could be a problem. We'll just have to hope for the best."

Slava wasn't finished. "We are also supposed to give them the cup of Khan Krum. We don't have it."

"Maddock has it, and if I know him, he'll probably turn up any minute. We just need to figure out a way to let him know what we're doing."

As if on cue, a waiter approached carrying a bottle of amber colored liquid on his tray. Bones couldn't decipher the Cyrillic writing on the label, which featured a powerful-looking ram, but he had seen enough booze in his lifetime to guess that it was some kind of whisky. The server placed the bottle on the table, along with three rocks glasses and a small dish of ice cubes.

Bones glanced over at Corey. "Did you order this?"

Before Corey could reply, the server explained, in halting English. "Is gift for you." He handed Bones a folded sheet of paper, which Bones regarded warily for a moment before opening.

"Is it from the kidnappers?" Corey asked.

Bones scanned the page which contained just a few lines of perfectly legible English. He broke into a relieved smile as he read it aloud. "'Sorry about the local brand. Couldn't get Wild Turkey. But as they say, don't judge a movie by its poster—JL.'"

"Who is JL?" asked Slava.

Bones regarded her thoughtfully for a moment before answering. "An old buddy of Maddock's. A computer geek. Maddock must have made contact with him, and this is his way of letting us know."

"It seems like a very cryptic way of doing that. Why not just call or send an email?"

Bones continued to watch her. "Obviously, Maddock doesn't trust the regular lines of communication. Our phones and computers may be compromised."

A frown creased Slava's forehead. "I assure you, my phone is not compromised. I have the very best security software."

Bones offered a helpless shrug. "What can I say? Jimmy's paranoid about stuff like that."

"So what are we supposed to do now?" asked Corey.

Bones pulled the bottle to him, unstoppered it, and waved it under his nose. "Not bad, but it's a little early in the day for the hard stuff." He replaced the lid and set the bottle down. "This is Jimmy's way of telling us that he knows we're here—or specifically, that I'm here. I vote we stay put until Jimmy gives us more information. Or until Maddock shows up."

He turned, hoping to signal the departing waiter to return, but instead spied a familiar if bedraggled figure entering the casino. "Speak of the devil," Bones muttered, and as Maddock joined them at the table, he added, "Didn't think we'd see you again for a while."

"Jimmy arranged a rideshare for me," Maddock explained. "Promised a big tip if the driver could get me here, ASAP. I think the guy thought he was Jason Statham, or something."

Bones pointed at the backpack slung over Maddock's shoulder. "You still have that, I see."

Maddock nodded. "Yep, and now we're going to get Max back."

"I don't know if you heard," said Corey, "but now the kidnappers want us to find the treasure, too. And they're only giving us three days to find it."

"That's not very much time. Especially since all we know for sure is that it isn't at Prohodna." Maddock turned his gaze to Slava. "Which makes me wonder why you sent us there in the first place, Miss Kostadinova."

He paused a beat, and then added, "Or should I call you Atanas?"

16

Slava tensed, as if about to flee, but then appeared to reconsider. Her demeanor softened, and her facial expression reflected confusion. "I don't know what you mean."

Bones leaned forward. "I think he means you're not as Hallmark Channel as you look."

Maddock nodded to Bones, pleased that his friend had picked up on the subtext of Jimmy's message. "When Jimmy tried to look up your phone number to see if the *mutri* had cloned your phone, he discovered that there isn't anyone named Slava Kostadinova at the Bulgarian Ministry of Tourism. There's a Svetla Kostadinova, but she doesn't look a thing like you."

"I can explain this—"

Maddock cut her off. "Which is odd, because the Ministry definitely paid for our flights, hotel rooms, rental car... the whole works, just like you said they did. He dug a little deeper and realized that someone had hacked into the Ministry's computers and used their accounts to bankroll this whole fiasco. Jimmy recognized the digital fingerprints left by the hacker."

He cocked his head sideways to look at her. "Jimmy says you're a legend. I think he's a little envious that I got to meet you face-to-face. I promised him I'd ask for your autograph, but first, you're going to tell me why you kidnapped Max, and then you're going to get him back from your gangster pals."

The blonde woman regarded him cautiously, her eyes occasionally darting left and right, which Maddock knew might signify either an attempt to come up with a plausible way to deny the accusations, or a visual survey of possible escape routes. But then her shoulders slumped in defeat. "This wasn't how it was supposed to happen."

Corey gasped. "So it's true? You're Atanas?" He snapped his fingers. "The alarm at the museum that distracted the guards... That was you, wasn't it? And the way you found the combination to the vault. How did I not notice?"

Maddock fought to maintain his stern expression. Of course, those were the details Corey would focus on. "Just how *was* it supposed to happen?"

"You weren't supposed to find anything at Tsarichina," she said.

The answer caught Maddock off guard. "What?"

"The only reason I brought Max there was so that he could prove once and for all that there was nothing at Tsarichina."

Maddock shook his head. "I don't understand. Why do you care if there's anything there?"

Slava took a deep breath, letting it out in a long sigh. "You know that my name isn't Kostadinova. I was born Stanislava Ionova."

"Ionova," Bones repeated, immediately grasping the significance. "One of the remote viewers at Tsarichina was named Ionova."

"Maria," Slava confirmed. "She was my mother. I was just five years old when she took her own life."

Maddock scrutinized her expression, but saw nothing to suggest that she was attempting to deceive. Instead, he saw the pain of an old wound, never healed. "This doesn't have anything to do with lost treasure, does it?"

She pursed her lips together. "I don't know. To answer, I must first tell you the true history of Operation:

Sun Ray. The story that Max told… The story that everyone today knows, is not the whole story. It begins with my grandfather, Colonel Stanislav Ionov, director of the Bulgarian defense ministry's division of psychic research.

"My grandfather was not merely a government official in charge of a speculative program. He was a true believer."

"Because of your mother."

Slava shook her head affirmatively. "But my mother wasn't really a psychic. She was…My mother was not well. Mentally. When she was very young, she had an imaginary playmate she called Kiki."

"Lots of kids have imaginary friends."

"Perhaps what you say is true, but in Bulgaria, even today, children who see people that aren't there are institutionalized. I don't know if my father started out believing that my mother was truly channeling a spirit, or if he was simply trying to protect her… and his own career from scandal… but I do know that he convinced her, intentionally or not, that she was special." Her voice dropped low, as if merely speaking the words was an ordeal. "Maybe that was good for her… I don't know. But then, when she was fourteen years old, she…" Her voice broke.

"She got pregnant with you," Maddock guessed.

Slava shook her head again. "When my grandfather realized that she was with child, he demanded to know who the father was. I think he suspected one of his junior officers had taken advantage of her, but my mother would only say that Kiki had given her a special blessing. I think the pregnancy was what truly sent her over the edge of madness. And my grandfather, too."

Despite the urgency of his need for answers,

Maddock found himself drawn into her story, and remained silent as she paused to blink away tears.

"I was never told any of this as a child. Grandfather only ever told me that my mother was a gifted psychic. But as I grew older and learned about mental illness, I realized the truth that he refused to admit to himself.

"Even that might not have mattered. So mama was a little kooky… So what, right? But then, one day, my grandfather was visited by a man named Dmitri Marinov, who claimed to have seen a vision of a Bulgarian folk hero—Vulchan Voivode—telling him that he was a descendant of Tsar Samuil, and that he should look for treasure in Tsarichina.

"Grandfather didn't know whether or not to believe Marinov, so he asked my mother to contact Kiki for confirmation. My mother said that Marinov was telling the truth, but told him to look in a different spot from the location Marinov had indicated. Grandfather presented the information to his superiors, who authorized him to begin searching Tsarichina for the buried treasure of Samuil.

"It was only to have been a small operation, but then one of the psychics from the program—Rumen Nikolov— came forward with wild claims involving extraterrestrial entities and forgotten civilizations. Nikolov claimed to be in contact with an alien spirit, and produced hundreds of pages of alien writing. He said that there was a lepton-ray weapon buried at Tsarichina, and that if it was not recovered in forty-eight hours, the world would be destroyed. When they did not find anything in two days' time, the message changed and changed again, and the government, desperate to possess the secret of an alien weapon, went along with it all.

"It was bad enough that Nikolov stole the operation

away from my grandfather, but when my mother claimed to be receiving information from Kiki that contradicted him, he attacked her. Not openly, of course. But he knew how fragile she was. Grandfather believed Nikolov was attacking her psychically, but I don't think there was anything supernatural about it."

"He gaslighted her," Corey murmured.

"He drove her to suicide," Slava said. "And then, after two years and millions wasted, he used her death to support his claim that the secret of Tsarichina was too dangerous to be revealed. And today? Today, Nikolov still claims to be in contact with the entity at Tsarichina. He built an entire career on it. Books. Lectures. He's earned millions. My mother killed herself. My grandfather's career and reputation were destroyed. But Nikolov? He's famous."

"And you became a computer geek," Bones put in.

"My mother and grandfather believed they could call on psychic powers and spirits for secret knowledge, but I developed a different sort of ability—I learned how to use computers so that I could learn the truth about what happened. That is how I discovered the back door into Tsarichina."

Maddock nodded slowly as understanding dawned. "You wanted to expose them as frauds. That's what you meant when you said we weren't supposed to find anything at Tsarichina."

"The discovery of the cup of Khan Krum would have strengthened Nikolov's reputation. Made him even more famous. I couldn't let that happen."

"So you went to the Bulgarian mob and convinced them to kidnap Max in exchange for the proof."

Corey shook his head. "Even without the cup, we've still got all the footage we shot."

"Easy enough for a master hacker to make that disappear," Bones remarked.

Corey gasped in horror.

"I was desperate," Slava said, lowering her gaze. "I didn't know what to do. I thought my plan would work. But Dragomirov—the gangster—must have learned about the treasure map in the cup from Max, and decided to take everything for himself. I tried to make him understand, but he won't listen to me anymore."

Maddock felt a measure of sympathy for her, but that did not excuse the choices she had made. "Did you tell Dragomirov that we were going to Prohodna?"

She nodded once. "No. I was supposed to be the only one to interact with you. And I only sent you there to get you out of the way. Send you on a wild goose chase."

"I wonder how many ways he has to track our movements." Maddock glanced over at Bones. "Did you spot any surveillance?"

"No, but if this guy is as connected as it sounds, he's probably got eyes everywhere. Especially here. Mobsters and casinos go together like flies and crap."

"It's going to be tough to hide our movements from him," Maddock said. He returned his attention to Slava. "Do you have any idea where he's keeping Max?"

Slava gave another miserable nod—Maddock had to keep reminding himself that it meant the opposite of what he thought. "He owns many properties in Sofia. Max might be at any one of them."

"So, the only way we get Max back is if we find that treasure."

Bones nodded. "We were thinking they might take the coins you found at Tsarichina. But if Max already told them about it, we're screwed."

Maddock considered this for a few seconds, then

shook his head. "The guy who originally claimed there was treasure at Tsarichina…"

"Marinov."

"He said he was visited by the spirit of a revolutionary hero, right?"

Slava shook her head. "Vulchan. The name means 'wolf.' He is sort of a Bulgarian Robin Hood."

"Is it possible that he's the one who left the cup and those coins in the cave at Tsarichina?"

She frowned. "If the legends about him are true, then yes, it is possible. He was said to have stolen treasures from the Ottoman Bey, and discovered troves of Thracian and Roman riches."

"So this Vulchan might have divided up the treasure. Put some of it in that cave at Tsarichina, and hid the rest somewhere else. He might have even been the one who left that message in the cup."

"Yes," Bones said, slowly. "And he's been dead at least a century or two."

"Exactly. And who do you go to when you need an answer from someone who's dead?"

"Uh… John Edward?"

Maddock chuckled. "You're on the right track, but I was thinking somebody a little closer to the problem." He turned to Slava. "What happened to Marinov?"

"As far as I know, his involvement ended when Rumen and Sirakov took over. He may even have died."

"Can you find out?"

"I should be able to." Slava hesitated before adding, "If you will let me use my laptop."

"Please do."

Slava took her computer from her bag and opened it. As she began typing, Bones leaned close to Maddock. "So you're really going to ask a psychic for advice?"

Maddock spread his hands. "What can I say? He said there was treasure there, and he was right."

"I found him," Slava announced. "He is still alive. He lives at a retirement home in the Vitosha municipality. Not far from the museum."

"We need to talk to him." Maddock stood and made ready to leave, but then glanced to the bottle at the center of the table. "Let's bring that along. It would be impolite to drop in unannounced without a gift."

17

Dmitri Marinov lived in a small, sparsely furnished apartment on the uppermost floor of the retirement home. The facility looked nice enough on the outside, a three-story building painted a cheerful red and yellow, with a well-tended garden area in back, but the interior was utilitarian and depressing.

Marinov was a wiry man who looked to be at least in his eighties. He was happy to have visitors, especially visitors with an offering of Black Ram whisky, but when Slava explained that the Americans accompanying her were making a documentary film about the Tsarichina excavation, his demeanor changed. His eyes narrowed warily, his utterances became more guarded.

"He asks why you have come to him," Slava said.

"Tell him that we know he was the one who had originally brought Tsarichina to the attention of the authorities. We want to hear that story, in his own words."

Slava dutifully translated Maddock's request, but Marinov's expression did not soften. He was silent for a while, as if trying to decide what answer would work best to rid himself of these bothersome guests. Finally, he spoke a few more words.

"It was a long time ago. I don't remember."

Maddock frowned. He had been hoping that the old man might be enticed with the prospect of being featured on Max's television show—he felt certain that Riddle would approve, provided of course, they were able to get him back in one piece. Marinov however, seemed immune to the allure of fame.

"Maybe he's camera shy," remarked Bones.

"Maybe." Maddock turned to Slava. "Tell him who you are."

"You mean, tell him that I am Maria Ionova's daughter?"

"And Colonel Ionov's granddaughter."

At the sound of the name, Marinov perked up, and he took a second look at Slava. When she spoke to him, his head shook slowly from side to side. There was recognition in his old eyes, but if anything, his countenance grew darker with barely restrained ire.

"He says I look just like her," Slava translated. "My mother, that is. But he blames my grandfather for what happened. For turning the search into a circus. For pushing him aside, and then making him an object of ridicule."

"Ouch," muttered Bones. "I guess we just ripped off a scab."

"At least he's talking to us," Maddock said.

Slava continued speaking in Bulgarian, with increasing ardor, but the old man remained unmoved, nodding his head to punctuate his refusal. Slava finally slumped her shoulders in defeat. "I told him that we want to tell the truth about what happened, to expose Nikolov as a fraud, but he refuses to help. He says he wishes he had never told anyone about his dream, and just wants to be left along to die in peace."

Maddock sighed. He had one last card to play, and if it didn't work, nothing would.

He unslung the backpack from his shoulder, opened it and removed the cup of Khan Krum, and then placed it on the table in front of Marinov.

Even before he could tell Slava what to say, the old man's face lit up. He rattled off a question.

Slava shook her head, affirmatively. "He asked if we found this at Tsarichina," she explained. "I told him we did."

The old man pounded his fist on the table in what Maddock took to be a gesture of vindication. Maddock slid the cup closer, gesturing that it was all right for Marinov to touch it, and as the old man's fingers curled around the stem, Maddock said, "Ask him if he's ready to talk, now."

Slava did, and this time, the old man met her gaze without obvious rancor. Slava did her best to keep up with the torrent of words that followed. "He says we already know the story. He says he had a dream in which Vulchan led him through the hills to a cave where there was treasure from the time of Tsar Samuil. 'Take this treasure, Dmitri,' Vulchan said. 'It is your birthright. Lead the Bulgars as once Samuil did.'"

The old man fell silent as Slava explained all this. When he resumed, a little of his earlier self-righteousness was evident in his tone.

"He says that he recognized the hills from a childhood visit to Tsarichina, and that is what he told my grandfather. But when they went to Tsarichina, they could not find the cave. My mother told my grandfather that they should look in a different place. Then the others came, talking about crazy things. They weren't even looking for the treasure. That's why they never found it."

"But you knew it was there," Maddock pressed.

The old man's eyes darted back and forth. "When they found nothing, I thought my dream was just that—a dream. Now I know that what I saw was true."

Maddock looked over at Slava. "I don't know if this will translate, so just do your best."

She shook her head once.

Maddock returned his gaze to Marinov. "Bull crap."

Slava choked in surprise, but then spoke a single word. "*Gluposti.*"

The old man bristled defensively, but Maddock didn't give him an opportunity to make a rebuttal. "You knew the treasure was there all right, but it wasn't because of any dream or psychic vision. You found something… A map or an old letter… Maybe even something from Vulchan himself, telling you to look for a cave in Tsarichina. I'll bet you turned the place upside down looking for it, and when you couldn't find it, you concocted that crazy story about having a psychic dream."

He paused a beat to let Slava catch up with the translation, then resumed, cutting off Marinov's retort. "You figured you could get the government to find it for you. Even if you didn't get to keep it, you'd be famous as the person who discovered it. Hell, people might even have bought your crazy story about being descended from Tsar Samuil."

He stopped again, watching the old man's eyes, seeing the truth of his accusations mirrored there. "But then everything went out of control," he went on. "You couldn't very well admit the truth. The best you could hope for was that they might stumble across the treasure, and then you would be vindicated. But it didn't happen. Until today.

"We found this cup along with a small chest of coins in a cave below the Tsarichina Hole." He tilted the cup so that Marinov could see the inscription inside the bowl. "But we think this is a map that may lead to even more treasure. If you know anything about that, now is the time to tell the truth."

The old man's frown continued to deepen as Slava translated, but when she finished, he leaned forward and peered into the cup. Maddock could see the old man's eyes moving as he read the inscription. Finally he sat back, and began speaking.

Slava smiled and turned to Maddock. "He says he will tell you what he knows, but only if you give him the credit for finding Vulchan's treasure."

Maddock grinned and stuck out his hand. "Deal."

Marinov didn't need to wait for a translation. He shook Maddock's hand and then rose from his chair and went over to a small bookcase in the corner of the room. After rummaging in a small box for a few minutes, he returned with a slim volume gripped in his gnarled hands. The red cloth cover was faded and tattered, the spine cracked and split, and when the old man opened it and placed it flat on the table, Maddock saw that several yellowed and brittle pages had come loose from the binding. Marinov flipped through them, revealing page after page of handwritten entries.

"This book has always been in my family," Slava said, translating his comments verbatim. "It is the record of Vulchan's fight against the Turks. It tells of how Vulchan found the treasure of Tsar Samuil. Some of it he gave to the people, but the rest he hid away, keeping the location a secret, even from his most trusted lieutenants. However, to ensure that the location would be remembered, even if Vulchan himself was killed, he described the location of a cave in the Balkan Mountains, north of Sofia.

"He did not say exactly where it was," the old man went on. "But his description of the area around the entrance was very detailed. In my family, we always knew that the place it described was Tsarichina, but in the exact spot where Vulchan's cave should have been, there was nothing. I searched for it when I was a young man, even though the Communists would have taken the treasure from me, but I never found the cave Vulchan described." He paused as if to reflect, and then added, "If ever there was a time of great need for Bulgaria, that was it."

"Maybe the entrance caved in," Corey suggested.

Slava shook her head. "It is possible. The Sofia valley has had many powerful earthquakes throughout history. It is a seismic hotspot."

Marinov continued. "Eventually, the Communists fell from power. That was when I came up with the idea to contact the authorities, claiming that I saw Vulchan in a vision. You know the rest.

"Vulchan wrote that to find the treasure, one would first have to find the cave. I always thought it meant that the treasure was in the cave, but now I think what he meant was that the map to the treasure—" He gestured to the skull cup on the table, "was hidden in the cave."

"That doesn't put us any closer to finding the treasure," Maddock countered. "We still don't know what the map is trying to tell us."

Marinov stared at him, but as Slava translated, a smile touched his lips.

"I know," he said, confidently, tapping his chest as he spoke. He then pointed to the inscription in the cup again. "Vulchan spoke often of having God's eyes upon him."

"Let me guess," Bones muttered. "Prohodna."

The old man's eyes flashed with recognition, but he nodded and uttered a negative, followed by a short declaration.

"No," Slava translated. "He was speaking of a church."

"Oh, well that narrows it down," Bones said. "You can't throw a frisbee in this town and not hit a church."

"But in the time of Vulchan," Slava went on, "there were no churches. The Ottomans either destroyed them all, or turned them into mosques."

As if sensing the gist of the conversation, the old man spoke again, and Slava quickly translated. "In 1858, an earthquake struck Sofia, nearly destroying the entire town. The Ottomans abandoned the city, and the Bulgarians were quick to reclaim the churches that had been converted into mosques. Repair work began almost immediately, paid for, in part at least, by Vulchan himself. He was especially fond of the Church of St. George, in old Serdica." She paused, then added, "I told you about it last night."

"The one in the courtyard behind the government buildings?"

Marinov spoke again. "Vulchan traveled all over Bulgaria, but when he came to Sofia, he always came to pray at the Church of St. George. In the sight of God. Those are the words he would always use. The treasure of Tsar Samuil is hidden there, and if we go to the church, this map will show us exactly where to look."

Maddock turned to Slava. "Can you bring up a floor plan of the church? Maybe give us an idea of what to expect?"

Slava produced her laptop, and in short order, displayed a gallery of images depicting the interior and exterior of the church. It was a small red brick structure, built around a central, cylindrical rotunda, capped with a low conical roof, and surrounded by the brick foundations of ancient Roman buildings that had not survived the march of time.

The interior was even more remarkable, adorned with numerous vividly painted and restored frescoes of saints and apostles. The most noteworthy of these occupied the upper reaches of the chapel which curled overhead like a capacious umbrella. Spaced at intervals around the circumference were large arched windows.

"Another dome," remarked Corey.

"Remind you of anything?" Bones said, nodding toward the cup. "What do want to bet that the lines inside the cup correspond to something on the ceiling of that church?"

"Or something on the floor," said Maddock. "Is there a three-sixty photo of the church?"

After a few keystrokes, the screen was filled with a virtual reality view of the church's interior.

"Hang on a sec," Corey said, and brought out his tablet. "I'm superimposing the scan I did of the cup onto the three-sixty of the church."

After a minute or two of fiddling with it, he placed it flat on the table. The screen showed the church ceiling again, along with a red outline that corresponded to the stylized skull sutures that crossed the interior of the cup.

Corey touched the edges of the screen and began sliding them back and forth. The red lines remained fixed, but the image of the church began to rotate as if it was being projected onto the inside of a beach ball. He continued turning the background, rolling the perspective down the walls and on to the floor of the chapel but nothing in the church seemed to align with the overlay.

"We're going about this wrong," Maddock said after a few fruitless minutes. "Does the church have a crypt?"

Slava did another quick search, then said. "No, but archaeologists did find evidence of an ancient Roman heating system called a *hypocaust*. It's a network of underground ducts that carry geothermal heat up from the underground hot springs. Most of the old ducts have long since collapsed, but if there was a vent inside the church, Vulchan might have cleared it out and used it to hide his treasure."

Marinov spoke up, prompting Slava to explain what they were doing. After she finished he gave a sagacious head shake.

"He says that sounds like something Vulchan would do," she explained.

"Is there a map of the ducts?" asked Maddock.

After a few more keystrokes, Slava shook her head. "Here!" she said, pointing at her screen, which now displayed a general site plan of the Serdica ruins. Running through several of the various square and rectangular plots were broken lines that branched off in different directions. "Here is the church," she explained, tapping a roughly cross-shaped structure in the middle of the screen. Her finger moved to a dotted line that transected the building. "One of the hypocaust ducts runs right under it."

Maddock stared at the plan for several seconds, then looked over at Corey's tablet, confirming his suspicions. "The lines in the cup match some of the hypocaust tunnels."

Corey took another look. "You're right. Let me just... find the site plan... There!"

He showed the tablet which now displayed the image Slava had found with the red tracery from the skull cup overlaid and scaled to match. As Maddock had predicted, the line in the cup perfectly matched the section of ancient ductwork that began under the church, but with a few conspicuous differences. The short branch-like extensions indicated junctions which continued in various directions, while the main line continued beyond what was indicated in the site plan.

"That's what the map is telling us," said Maddock. "If we can find our way into that duct and follow to the end, we'll find the treasure. There's got to be an opening inside the church."

Corey navigated back to the panoramic image of the church, turning the image a full three-sixty. He stopped when it showed the back of the nave, which was dominated by an ornate wooden screen, adorned with painted icons. "That altarpiece could be covering the entrance to an old crypt," he suggested.

"It's called an iconostasis," said Slava. "But I think you're right. If there is an entrance to the hypocaust, that would be the place to put it."

"We're going to have to get in there and move the furniture," Maddock said.

Bones scratched his chin. "It's pretty public. Worse than the Eyes of God cave. We start poking around, and people are going to notice."

Maddock turned to Slava again. "We're going to need your help with this."

"Me? What can I do?"

"Find a way to get us some time by ourselves in there. I'm sure you'll think of something. Remember, you're not just Slava from the tourist ministry. You're Atanas, the hacker."

"If this mobster, Dragomiov, really does have eyes everywhere," said Bones, "he's going to wonder what we're up to in there."

Maddock nodded slowly. "We're only going to get one chance to get in there. Treasure or not, we have to get Max back before Dragomirov realizes where we're looking."

"How do you propose to accomplish that magic trick?"

"I'm not sure yet," Maddock said, though the first seeds of a plan were already starting to sprout. "I guess I'll have to think of something."

18

"**What are they** doing in there?" Dragomirov rumbled from the front passenger seat of the unmarked delivery pan—the same vehicle he had used to abduct Max Riddle the previous evening. The van was parked half a block away from the red and yellow building where Dane Maddock and his little band of treasure hunters had gone after leaving the hotel.

"Want me to go in and find out?" asked Nikolay from behind the steering wheel.

It had been a rhetorical question, but Dragomirov considered the offer. Why had Maddock and his crew come here, to this old pensioners' refuge? Why weren't they out looking for the treasure?

Maybe it was time to remind Maddock of what was at stake.

"Not just yet," he said, taking out his phone. He dialed a number. The phone rang once and then Krasimir picked up.

Dragomirov didn't bother with a greeting. "I want you to do something for me. Go downstairs to our guest and cut off one of his ears. Then bring it here to me."

Krasimir gave an eager chuckle. "I'll take care of it. Where are you?"

"I'll text you the address," Dragomirov said. The old warehouse where they were keeping Riddle was only about a fifteen-minute drive from the retirement home. The ear would still be warm when he handed it to Maddock.

As he was in the process of sending his location to Krasimir however, the other phone in his pocket—Riddle's phone—began to vibrate. A sly smile curled his lips as he accepted the call.

"You are wasting time," he said. "Tell Dane Maddock that his friend is going to pay dearly for this delay."

He expected to hear the woman from the tourist office, but instead the answering voice was male, speaking English. "Am I speaking to Boyan Dragomirov?"

Dragomirov felt a surge of panic. How had Maddock learned his identity? He took a deep breath, then replied in the same language

"Ah, Mr. Maddock. I was just going to send you a message."

"Well, I've got a message for you, so shut up and listen."

Dragomirov felt heat flash across his face, but before he could articulate his rage, Maddock spoke again. "I know where the treasure is. If you want it, you're going to have to follow my instructions to the letter. First, you're going to let me talk to Max."

"No. I'm not going to do that. What I'm going to do—" A double-beep signaled that the call had ended.

Dragomirov's nostrils flared. How dare this American treat him this way?

I'm going to make you suffer before I kill you, he thought. *But first....*

He took a deep breath to bring his ire under control, and then called back. Maddock picked up immediately.

"I told you to shut up and listen," Maddock said. "You don't get anything from me until I know that Max is alive and well. And I do mean *well*. If he's got so much as a skinned knee, you'll never see any of the treasure. I'll turn every bit of it over to the government, and I'll do it very publicly so that your cronies won't be able to pilfer it. And if you think I won't go through with it because he's my friend, think again. I don't even like him that much."

Dragomirov drummed his fingers on the armrest of his seat, trying to decide how seriously to take the threat. "Just a moment," he said, and then without hanging up on Maddock, called his brother on the other phone. "Krasimir, have you already done what I asked you to do?"

There was a long and somewhat worrying pause. "I was just about to," Krasimir admitted, a little guiltily.

Dragomirov breathed out a relieved sigh. "Don't. Change of plan. I want you to put your phone on speaker, and let him talk."

Without waiting for Krasimir to acknowledge, Dragomirov placed both phones on speaker and held them close. "Mr. Maddock. You may speak to Mr. Riddle now."

Riddle was the first to speak. "Dane? Are you there?"

"I'm here Max," answered Maddock. "You okay?"

"I've been better. I'll be honest, man. I'm a little freaked out."

"Everything's going to be okay, Max. Just hang on a little while longer."

"That's enough," Dragomirov broke in, and then added in Bulgarian, "Krasimir, don't do anything until I call you back." He ended the call, and then addressed Maddock. "There. You have your proof of life. And if you want to keep him alive and well, you had better deliver the treasure to me soon."

"That's not how this is going to work," Maddock countered.

"Don't test me, Maddock."

"We both know what you're really planning. As soon as you get what you want, you're going to kill Max, maybe kill us all… No witnesses, no loose ends, right?"

"If you believe that, why are we talking?"

Maddock ignored the question. "Kidnapping an American television personality was a really dumb idea. Did you think you could just disappear him, and there wouldn't be any fallout?"

Dragomirov frowned. In fact, he had believed exactly that. But that was before Maddock had learned his identity.

"But your big mistake," Maddock went on, "was double-crossing Bulgaria's most notorious hacker."

"Atanas," Dragomirov muttered. "Damn him."

"Your friends in high places won't be able to protect you. Not with the evidence we've already got. The smart thing for you to do would be to set Max free and walk away. But we both know you're not going to do that. So I'm going to make you a counter-offer."

The mobster's frown deepened. He was in unfamiliar territory now, and he didn't like it one bit. "I'm listening."

"First, we're going to meet face to face. And you're going to bring Max with you. Then, if you do exactly as I say, I'm going to take you straight to the treasure."

Dragomirov was immediately suspicious. "I don't understand why you would do that. What's in it for you?"

"Like I said, we both know you're not going to walk away empty-handed. I have no use for the treasure. It's not like I was going to get to keep it."

Dragomirov's fingers thumped against the armrest again. *He's trying to trick me. I know it. But what's his game?*

He smiled. *I can play games, too.*

"All right, Maddock," he said. "We'll do this your way."

"Good." There was a sound of muffled voices, as if Maddock was covering the phone, and then, he spoke clearly again. "There's a McDonald's near the Banya Bashi mosque. We'll meet there in two hours. Just you and Max. Leave the rest of your goons behind."

McDonald's? The mobster rolled his eyes. *Typical Americans.*

"Don't be late," Maddock added, and then ended the call.

"Of all the places we could have picked for a meeting," Bones said, setting a slightly grease-stained paper bag atop the outdoor café table. "You chose Mickey-Dees."

He settled into a metal chair opposite Maddock and began removing the bag's contents—a sandwich wrapped in paper, a red cardboard sleeve stuffed with French fries, and a handful of napkins.

Maddock shrugged. "It's close to where we're going, and easier to pronounce than any of the local places." He watched with mild fascination as Bones first peeled back the paper to expose a double-decker hamburger, and then took an enormous bite. "I don't know why you're complaining. You didn't have to order anything."

"I've set a life goal to eat a Big Mac in every country on earth," he said, mumbling through a partially chewed mouthful. "Just to see if they're the same everywhere you go."

Maddock shook his head. "Why do I suddenly feel like I'm trapped in a movie?"

Bones swallowed and grinned. "The only problem is you've got the roles mixed up. I'd be Sam Jackson because he's the cool one, and you'd be Travolta because he's the gigantic douche-nozzle."

Maddock affected a look of confusion, "Oh... You thought I was making a *Pulp Fiction* reference. No, I was talking about *Super-Size Me.*"

Bones flashed a one-fingered salute, then jammed half-a-dozen golden fries into his mouth.

Culinary considerations notwithstanding, the restaurant was the perfect place from which to launch the next phase of the plan to get Riddle back from his captors. The McDonald's was located only about a block away from the Serdica ruins and the complex of government buildings which surrounded the Church of St. George. It was also a very public location, where Dragomirov would hopefully think twice about making a display of force.

Despite the light-hearted banter, both men were acutely aware of just how dangerous the meeting with Dragomirov would be. They had faced danger together too many times to count, and knew all too well the truth of the old adage about the battle plan being the first casualty of war. Maddock didn't believe for a second that the mobster would comply with the demand to come alone, nor did he think Dragomirov would allow Max Riddle to just go free. Maddock's plan would even the odds a little, but everything hinged on actually finding the treasure. If it wasn't there... If they had misread the clues, or worse, someone else had pillaged the trove long before... There was no telling how Dragomirov might react, but Maddock didn't dare to hope that the Bulgarian would cut his losses and slink away.

As Bones was polishing off the last of his fries, a white delivery van rolled to a stop in front of them.

"Showtime," Maddock murmured as the sliding door opened to reveal three men in the rear cargo area. Two he recognized from the encounter atop Prohodna cave—the middle-aged man with the gun, whom Maddock surmised was probably Dragomirov himself, and his butterfly-knife flipping younger counterpart. Riddle was the third man.

Only Dragomirov moved, getting out and crossing to the table where Maddock and Bones sat.

"Mr. Maddock. We meet again. At Prohodna, you ran off before we could talk."

"You didn't seem that interested in talking," Maddock shot back. He glanced down at his watch. "You cut it close. And I guess you weren't paying attention when I said just you and Max. Have him get out, and then tell the rest of your boys to get lost."

"I don't think so," Dragomirov replied. "There are two of you, so I think it only fair that my brother Krasimir join us." He glanced back at the van and made a come-along gesture. Riddle and the other man got out, the latter gripping the former's biceps. As soon as they were on the sidewalk, the door closed and the van drove away.

Maddock made a show of looking perturbed at this deviation from his instructions, but secretly he was pleased that the mobster hadn't insisted on keeping more of his men. He turned his gaze to Riddle. "You okay, Max?"

Riddle nodded, looking relieved despite the fact that Krasimir had his arm in a vise-grip. "I'm really glad to see you guys."

Maddock nodded. "This will all be over soon, I promise."

"Be careful about making promises, Mr. Maddock," interjected Dragomirov. "Mr. Riddle is still my guest, and will remain so until you take me to the treasure."

Riddle's head came up at the mention of the word. "Treasure? So there really is a treasure?"

"There is," Maddock said, and then silently amended, *I hope.*

Dragomirov uttered a growl of displeasure. "You are stalling. Where is it?"

Maddock checked his watch again. "Wait for it…"

The shrill wail of a siren abruptly rose above the low hum of traffic, and as it grew louder with each passing second, Dragomirov's look of irritation gave way to one of concern, and then anger.

"What have you done?" he raged at Maddock. His hand slid down to the hem of his polo shirt and the poorly concealed handgun beneath it. "I warned you not to call the police."

Maddock raised a hand to forestall him. "They aren't coming for you."

"Take a load off," Bones said, gesturing to one of the empty chairs. "This will take a few minutes. You've probably got time to grab a bite if you want."

Dragomirov however remained on guard as the siren noise reached a crescendo. A red fire engine roared past them from the north, continuing along to the next intersection where it screeched to a halt almost directly in front of the statue of Sveta Sofia, but it was not the only source of the tumult. In a matter of minutes, dozens of police cars and fire trucks arrived, spreading out along the perimeter surrounding the entire city block containing the Largo Complex and the Hotel Balkan. A swarm of first responders, many of whom had donned gas masks and other items of personal protective equipment, spread out, erecting barricades to block all approaches to the area.

"What is going on?" asked Dragomirov, suspiciously.

Maddock leaned forward and lowered his voice to a conspiratorial whisper. "A few minutes ago, the computers that monitor the underground natural gas lines registered a drop in pressure, localized to this general area." He gestured down the street. "The authorities are evacuating everyone until the possible leak can be investigated.

"Of course, there isn't actually a leak. It's just a computer glitch, but they won't figure that out until after they've done a physical inspection of the lines, which will take a couple hours." He reached down and picked up a large hockey bag which had been resting under his chair and placed it on the table. He stood to unzip it and began removing its contents—four neatly folded sets of gray work coveralls, four half-face respirators in unopened plastic bags, and four official-looking laminated cards.

Dragomirov regarded the objects from beneath a raised eyebrow. "What are these?"

"The short answer is: camouflage." Maddock peeled a pair of coveralls from the stack and pushed it across to the mobster. "Here. This one's for you."

"I don't understand."

Maddock glanced over at Bones, who just rolled his eyes. "We're going in there," Maddock explained, pointing toward the barricaded area. "These passes identify us as inspectors from the gas company."

"What if the police stop and question us?"

"In my experience, if you look like you know where you're going, people tend to leave you alone. If not, you can explain it to them."

"Me?"

"You're the only one of us who speaks Bulgarian. Just tell them who we are… Our cover story, obviously… And if they still have questions, tell them to call their supervisor, who will confirm that we have authorization to be there. We've already backstopped these IDs." He passed another set of equipment to Riddle. "You're going in with us, Max." He then looked at Krasimir. "Sorry, we don't have an extra pair. Looks like you'll have to stay behind."

Krasimir bristled at this. "No. One of you can stay."

Maddock fought the impulse to shake his head, knowing that it would be misinterpreted. "Sorry, but that's not going to happen. If you want the treasure, you do it our way."

Dragomirov was more measured in his response. "And if we refuse?"

Maddock shrugged. "Then nobody goes in, and you don't get the treasure. This is the only chance we're going to have, but we have to do it now, while everyone is cleared out. We won't be able to pull this stunt off twice. It's now or never."

Krasimir pointed at Riddle. "Leave him, then."

For just a second, Riddle appeared to brighten at the idea, but then his forehead creased with a frown. Maddock didn't give him a vote. "No. I'm not letting Max out of my sight. This isn't a negotiation. The clock is ticking."

The young *mutri* started to protest again, but Dragomirov forestalled him. "It's okay, Krasimir. We'll do it their way." He picked up the coveralls, shook them out, and held them up for inspection. "This had better be worth the trouble, Maddock."

Krasimir fumed as he watched his brother and the other three men pass unhindered through the police barricades. The policemen standing guard at the wooden barrier had not even given the men a second look. In their disguises—anonymous coveralls, respirators and paper painter's hats—it was impossible to tell who was who, save for the big American Indian who towered over the others.

Krasimir clenched his fists in impotent rage. He needed to find a way past the barricades and the policemen. But how?

He started moving toward the outskirts of the closed area, searching for some weakness in the perimeter where he might be able to slip through unnoticed. The concentration of police officers was greatest on the main streets and along the detour route, but the side streets were either unguarded or monitored at a distance by roving police officers and firefighters. Unfortunately, getting past the barricade was only part of the problem. Once inside, he would immediately attract the attention of those patrols.

He needed a disguise, something better than coveralls and a respirator.

A smile touched his lips as a solution presented itself. Fifty feet away, on the other side of the barricades, a lone firefighter stood at the rear of a parked fire engine. Though the man had his back to Krasimir, and was mostly hidden by his long turnout coat, it was plainly evident that he was relieving himself against the truck's rear tire. Krasimir waited until he saw the man's shoulders shake a couple times, and then called out to him.

The firefighter's head bobbed and then swiveled around until his gaze finally settled on Krasimir, who prompted him to come closer with a sly wave. The man frowned back, refusing to move.

Krasimir tried again. "Hey, what's going on?"

"Gas leak," shouted the firefighter. "Nobody can go in until they check it."

Krasimir cupped a hand to his ear, signaling that he couldn't make out the words. The firefighter began to repeat the message in an even louder shout, but then heaved a sigh and headed over to the barricade. "Gas leak," he repeated when they were almost face to face. "The area has been evacuated until further notice."

"Oh, man, that's terrible." Krasimir affected a look of grave disappointment. He glanced past the man, trying to think of a plausible reason to surreptitiously enter the restricted zone, and spied the gilt letters on the front window of the bottom floor of the hotel. "I need to pick something up from the casino. It's really important." And then, with a raised eyebrow, he added, "Family business, if you know what I mean."

The man's frown deepened. Clearly, he did know. "Sorry, friend, but you'll have to wait like everyone else."

Krasimir glanced up and down the street, checking to make sure that no one was observing the exchange, and then dipped a hand into his pocket. He drew out a fat roll of cash, from which he peeled off two fifty-lev notes. "Maybe I can persuade you to look the other way."

The man's expression twisted into a sneer. "You thugs. You think you can just throw money around and get whatever you want."

Krasimir peeled off two more notes, and then two more, but the man's countenance only grew darker. It wasn't a princely sum—three hundred lev was only about a hundred and fifty American dollars—but Krasimir knew the amount was irrelevant. This was a point of pride for the firefighter. Later, no doubt, he would brag to his comrades about how he had stood up to a *mutri* punk, and told him what to do with his filthy money.

That was fine with Krasimir. He had better uses for it, anyway.

He carefully returned the notes to his roll and shoved in back into his pocket, discreetly drawing out something else instead. "Look," he said, trying to keep an even tone. "I get it. You're an honorable man. I am, too. Maybe we got off on the wrong foot." He leaned closer to the man, as if to whisper something intimate. "There is something I need to show you."

As he said it, he squeezed the split-handles of his butterfly knife, releasing the spring-loaded catch, and then with a practiced flick of the wrist, opened the knife, one-handed. The motion caught the firefighter's eye, but before he could fully process what he was seeing, Krasimir drove the long, narrow blade straight up into the soft flesh under above the man's Adam's apple.

The man reflexively tried to pull away, but Krasimir brought his free hand up, palming the top of his victim's helmet, in order to ram the knife deeper still. With his windpipe severed, the man quickly asphyxiated, drowning in his own blood, and as shock set in, his struggles ceased altogether. Krasimir lowered the lifeless form to the ground, removed his knife and wiped it clean, and then dragged the firefighter into a nearby alley. There, he stripped off the man's helmet and turnout gear, and pulled it on over his own clothes. The inside of the fire-resistant jacket was wet and sticky with fresh blood, but there was hardly any visible on the black exterior. When he was fully kitted out in the firefighting gear, Krasimir dragged his victim behind some trash cans.

"You should have just taken the money," he said, as he dumped the contents of one refuse bin out to cover the body. Then, with one last check to make sure his crime had not been observed, he headed back to the barricade.

19

Once they were beyond the direct line of sight of anyone watching from outside the cordon, Maddock and the others removed the awkward respirators. The streets were eerily desolate, like the scene of some apocalyptic plague.

"A lot of folks are going to be mighty pissed if they figure out that we're responsible for the bogus alarm," Bones remarked.

"Hopefully, that won't happen until we're long gone." Maddock opened his bag and brought out the quadcopter. "Corey, I'm activating the drone, now. Are you receiving?"

Corey's voice sounded in both men's Bluetooth enabled earpieces. "Five by five."

Bones rolled his eyes. "What does that even mean?" he whispered.

Maddock shrugged. "I think he heard it from a TV show." He took a step back as the four rotor blades began to whir. A moment later, the copter lofted into the air, rising to a height of nearly fifty feet, where it hovered, turning slowly to get a panoramic perspective. The drone then zoomed away, surveying the route they had earlier reconnoitered on Google Earth.

"You're all clear," Corey said. "There's no one between you and the church."

Dragomirov had kept quiet during their walk, but now he spoke up. "Church? The treasure is in the Church of St. George? That explains why you had to clear the area."

"It's not in the church," Maddock said quickly, lest the mobster conclude that he no longer needed them.

"The church is just the starting point."

Maddock led the way around to the south side of the complex where a narrow passage which connected the relatively modern environs outside the Largo Complex to the ruins surrounding the old church. They picked their way through the maze of half walls and exposed foundations, and crossed to the church entrance. Despite Corey's assurance that they were completely alone, Maddock breathed a sigh of relief when the doors of the church closed behind them.

There were no pews in the rotunda, just an open floor of dark polished stone. At the back of the enclosure stood the ornate wooden iconostasis. While Dragomirov and Riddle looked on, Maddock knelt down and inspected the floor around its base. "Doesn't look like it's been moved recently. If ever."

"That's good, right?" replied Bones.

Maddock shrugged. "I guess we'll find out."

He circled around the screen and found a stable upright post. Lowered his shoulder to it, and began pushing. At first, nothing happened, but after a few seconds, the iconostasis began moving, scraping loudly across the floor.

"There's a trapdoor!" exclaimed Riddle.

Maddock manage to hide a look of relief. He didn't know what he would have done if there had been only bare floor under the iconostasis, but fortunately there was a rusty metal plate, about two feet across and flush with the floor.

"The treasure is down there?" Dragomirov asked. There was an eagerness in his voice—a hunger.

"Slow your roll," Bones said. "That is the entrance to a hypocaust. It's basically an old Roman HVAC system. There's a whole maze of ductwork down there, and we're the ones with the map, so don't get any ideas."

Maddock gave his friend a grateful nod. He did not doubt that Dragomirov would eventually turn on them, and had planned accordingly, but his strategy was contingent on actually finding the treasure first.

He reached into his bag and produced a small pry bar—another acquisition from the same hardware store where they had purchased the coveralls and respirators. Working one end of the chisel under the metal sheet, he was able to raise it and slide it out of the way, revealing an opening. Although the hole was large enough to accommodate even someone of Bones' size it only appeared to be a few feet deep. The floor itself was about twelve inches thick, but below that, there was only empty space extending out in every direction, like the crawlspace under a typical house.

Maddock donned his headlamp and a pair of leather work gloves before lowering himself into the passage. There were several upright pillars, spaced at regular intervals, supporting the floor. Further out, his light illumed the foundations walls. According to the site plan, there would be hypocaust ducts to the east and west, and if their speculation about the map was correct, the treasure would be found by heading east. He oriented himself in that direction and began crawling until he found the small opening. Warm air wafted out of it, just a faint echo of the heat that the hypocaust had once channeled throughout the ancient complex.

A glance back showed three headlamps bobbing in the darkness beneath the church and headed his way. Without a word, Maddock lowered himself onto his belly, and crawled into the passage.

After about twenty feet, he reached a junction. Recalling the pattern on the interior of Krum's cup, he ignored the passages branching off to the left and right, and continued forward. When he had cleared the intersection, he looked back and saw Dragomirov crawling after him.

Although they had discussed the order of movement, Maddock had placed an unspoken dilemma before the mobster. If he followed right behind Maddock, he would have Bones and Riddle behind him, which would put him at something of a disadvantage. On the other hand, if he brought up the rear, the other three might be able to lay in an ambush. Maddock was pleased that Dragomirov had chosen the former course of action for reasons that had nothing to do with any plan to physically overpower the man.

The journey into the hypocaust proceeded almost exactly as Maddock had anticipated. It was a testament to the engineering prowess of the ancient Romans that the tunnel had survived the centuries more or less intact, especially considering the region's history of seismic activity. The only real surprise was the heat. The ancient ductwork reminded him of being inside an endless pizza oven. It was an especially apt analogy as the air temperature seemed to increase a degree or two every few feet. It wasn't unbearable by any means, but in the close confines, even a change of a few degrees felt stifling.

He reached a second intersection, and recalling the course indicated by the map, took a left turn. Dragomirov was still following close on his heels. Maddock took the next turn to the right and continued on for another twenty feet until the passage took a bend to the left. According to the map, the passage also should have continued forward to what he hoped would be the treasure chamber, but that passage had not appeared on the site plan, and there was no sign of it here.

Maddock shone his light on the wall directly before him, looking for some indication of a hidden passage, but it looked no different than the rest of the hypocaust. There were no loose bricks, no breaks or seams in between. If there was a passage continuing forward, it had been bricked up long ago.

"Why do you stop?" asked Dragomirov. His voice was muffled but there was a distinct tone of irritation.

"We're supposed to go forward here," Maddock replied. "Somebody blocked the passage we're supposed to take."

He did not add that he took this as a hopeful sign. It made sense that Vulchan would have sealed the passage to hide his treasure. The fact that it was still sealed up a century and a half later meant that nobody had come along afterward and removed it.

"So what do we do?" growled the mobster.

"We make our own passage," Maddock answered, taking out his pry bar again. He worked the chisel-tip into a mortar joint, scraping it repeatedly in the crevice surrounding one of the bricks.

"Better hurry," Dragomirov said. "It's getting damn hot in here."

Maddock didn't need the admonition. His coveralls were soaked through with perspiration, and the exertion of trying to break through the wall was only making matters worse. Fortunately, the old lime mortar crumbled under the assault, and in a matter of just a few minutes, he had loosened the wall's hold on the brick enough that a hard blow fractured the remaining bits of mortar holding it in place, and with a little wiggling, he was able to work it free. As he did, a blast of hot, humid air rushed out of the dark hole he had opened.

"There's a void here," he announced. Judging by the

volume of air that had been exchanged with the breakthrough, it was more than just a small recess. "The passage keeps going."

He resumed attacking the wall with his pry bar, loosening more bricks until the hole was big enough to crawl through. Beyond the wall, the hypocaust duct continued, exactly as the map in the skull cup had indicated it would, but then, after another thirty feet or so, the passage began to slope downward. The degree of the descent was significant enough that Maddock had to brace himself with the heels of his hands keep from sliding. Heat radiated up through the brick floor, forcing him to keep moving in order to minimize time spent in contact with the hot surface. He was pretty sure that, despite the protection of the leather pads over his palms, he was already well on the way to first-degree burns.

But then, just when he was seriously considering calling it quits, the descent flattened out as the hypocaust tunnel opened into a larger chamber. Grateful to finally have a chance to give his hands and knees a break from the constant slow cooker, Maddock immediately got to his feet. It was only then, as his headlamp came up to illuminate more of the room, that he realized his light was being reflected back at him in a thousand tiny golden pinpoints of light.

"My God," said Dragomirov, rising to his feet right behind Maddock. "Samuil's treasure. It's real."

As Riddle and Bones joined them, adding the illumination of their headlamps, the magnitude of the discovery became fully apparent.

The chamber was large and roughly square—about twenty feet long and almost as wide, with a low, barrel-vault ceiling that was just barely high enough to allow Maddock to stand fully erect only if he stood exactly centered between the walls. Bones was forced to slouch a little in order to stand upright. There was an arched opening at the opposite end of the chamber, which was presumably the original means of entrance and egress.

To either side were enormous piles of gold coins, surely numbering into the tens, if not hundreds of thousands. They lay heaped against the walls, along with the mostly rotted remains of the chests that had once contained them. There were other items as well—cut stones, jewelry, statues of marble and bronze. Some of the latter were encrusted with oxidation, but Maddock did not doubt that even those pieces would be judged priceless. While he couldn't begin to make even a lowball estimate of the worth of the treasure, on the value of the gold alone, it had to be worth billions.

"This isn't just a treasure," Maddock said. "It's a treasury."

Riddle, who had been uncharacteristically quiet since his conditional liberation, found his voice again. "This is fantastic." He knelt over a heap of glittering discs. "These coins are just like the ones we found at Tsarichina."

"There's no way that Vulchan dude brought all this stuff down here through that passage," Bones said. "Not by himself."

Riddle gestured down the length of the hall. "Maybe he used the front door."

"Then why make a map that shows the passage from the church?" Bones shook his head.

Dragomirov swung his gaze toward Bones. "Vulchan Voivode? How is he a part of this?"

"He's the one who drew the map on Krum's cup," Bones explained. "And I don't think he hid the treasure here. I think it was here all along."

Maddock was inclined to agree with his friend. "I think you're right. Remember what Slava told us about Samuil? How he was surrounded by his enemies at the end? He probably didn't want to risk moving the royal treasury, so he hid it all down here, and then sealed off the entrance."

"Maybe we can unseal it?" suggested Dragomirov.

Maddock shot him a sidelong glance. The mobster sounded almost as if he regarded them as partners in the endeavor. Whether that was a calculation on his part, or if he had merely gotten caught up in the moment, Maddock couldn't say, but he knew better than to trust this apparent shift in their relationship. "Doesn't hurt to check," he replied.

As he started down the length of the vault, he became aware of a strange, low-frequency hum in the air, growing louder as he approached the arch.

"You hear that?" Bones asked from right behind him.

"Yeah. I know I've heard something like it before, but…" He shook his head. "Maybe we're underneath the tram line, or something."

"Nah. It's more like a waterfall, or rapids."

"That's exactly it." He snapped his fingers as the revelation led to another. "The hot springs. They must flow nearby."

Bones swiped a hand across his forehead and then flung beads of perspiration against the brick wall. The dark spots vanished almost instantly. "You think? It's like a friggin' crawdad boil in here."

"No kidding." He glanced back at Dragomirov, and lowered his voice. "I think it's just about time to get out of the kitchen."

The noise kept building to a low rumble as he neared

the arch, but as his light shone through, what it illumed almost made him forget about both the sound and the treasure.

"I guess that answers that," he said,

The room beyond was more like a long walk-in closet than a passage. It was about ten feet wide and twenty feet deep, with no other visible exits, but that wasn't the strangest thing about it. In the glow of his light, it looked as if the chamber was covered with thick white ice.

It wasn't ice, of course, but the glistening white substance that seemed to ooze from between the bricks, running down the walls to puddle on the floor like molten candle wax, looked remarkably like icicles hanging off a gutter in winter. The back wall was almost completely covered in the translucent material.

"That's not something you usually see in a church basement," mused Bones.

"Flowstone," Maddock murmured.

"What's that?" asked Riddle.

"It's a type of mineral formation. It's caused when water carries dissolved minerals through tiny fissures in rock. Or in this case, through the cement mortar holding the bricks together. The water evaporates, leaving behind mineral growths. Same principle as stalactites and stalagmites, only flowstone usually forms against walls. If I had to guess, I'd say this is travertine. It's a type of flowstone you usually find near hot springs."

"I guess now we know why Vulchan didn't come in through the front door," added Bones.

Riddle probed one of the smaller extrusions. With a little effort, he succeeded in snapping off a piece about the same size as his pinkie finger. "It's brittle. Maybe we could break through."

Maddock shook his head. "I don't think that would

be wise. There's a hot spring just behind these walls. If we start messing with it, there's a chance we might break the dam and flood this whole place."

Riddle dropped the travertine icicle and retreated a step.

"The Roman engineers who excavated these chambers would have known better than to put them so close to an active hot spring," Maddock went on. "I don't think it's an accident that this passage is sealed off. I think after Samuil moved his treasury down here, he bricked up the passage and then diverted a spring to fill in behind it. What better way to keep it safe from his enemies."

"And his friends," added Bones.

"Well, we're not getting out that way." Maddock made a show of checking his watch, and nodded to Bones, silently communicating that the moment of truth had arrived. He faced Dragomirov. "We kept our end of the bargain," he said. "Samuil's treasure, as promised. Now, the three of us are going to walk away. If you're smart, you'll do the same. You don't want to be down here when the authorities lift the cordon."

The mobster started, as if only now remembering everything that had led up to this point. For a few seconds, he could only gape at Maddock, as if struggling to comprehend what he had just been told. But then, he did the thing that Maddock had both expected and dreaded.

Tearing open his coveralls, Dragomirov reached down to his waistband, drew his pistol, and aimed it at Maddock. "You aren't going anywhere," he snarled.

"Wow," Bones deadpanned. "I did not see that coming."

"Don't be stupid," Maddock said, projecting a bravado that was not entirely genuine. "We knew you'd pull a stunt like this and we took precautions."

A glimmer of uncertainty flashed in Dragomirov's eyes, but he shrugged it off. "I have friends in the police department. They will believe me before they believe your hacker friend."

"They'll believe their own eyes." Maddock reached up and tapped the side of his headlamp where he had affixed a small GoPro Hero.

"Smile," Bones said. "You're on Candid Camera."

"We've been broadcasting the whole time. Not only that, but our *hacker friend* is going to send the footage viral if we don't make it back. The whole world is going to know that Samuil's treasure is down here, and we found it." He glanced over at Riddle. "How's that for great television?"

Riddle managed a nervous chuckle.

"We can edit this part out," Maddock went on. "Make you look like a partner in the discovery. That's got to be worth something. Kill us, and you won't even get that."

Dragomirov seemed to be at a loss for words, but then he nodded once. "No. You might be recording with that camera, but there's no way your signal is getting out. Not from down here."

"Ordinarily, you'd be right," said Bones. "The GoPro uses a Wi-Fi network for upload. Short range, and more or less line of sight transmission. That's why I left a trail of these." He held up a cheap-looking mobile phone. "They're networked together to bounce the signal all the way home."

"I told you," Maddock said. "We expected this."

"It's like that old fable about the scorpion," Bones added. "You couldn't help yourself. It's just your nature to be a douche-canoe."

Dragomirov nodded again. "No. You're bluffing.

Trying to trick me."

Maddock shrugged. "You want proof? Bones, put it on speaker."

Bones thumbed the screen of the burner phone. "Corey, my man. Are you digging the show?"

Maddock waited for Corey's reply.

And waited.

The anxiety drained from Dragomirov's face as the silence grew. A cold knot of dread twisted Maddock's gut. He knew that their daisy chain of repeaters had worked because Corey had signaled back every time Bones, bringing up the rear, had activated another burner phone.

So why wasn't Corey acknowledging now?

"Corey, don't worry about trying to come up with something clever. Just let us know that you're receiving. Five by five, remember?"

A new voice filled the chamber, but it wasn't Corey. "Save your breath. He can't hear you."

20

All eyes, including Dragomirov's, shifted back to the mouth of the hypocaust passage where a man—a firefighter, judging by his attire—was rising to his feet. The man's face was familiar, but it wasn't until a smiling Dragomirov spoke his name that Maddock recognized him.

"Krasimir. Perfect timing. How did you find us?"

The phony fireman grinned and then held up his hand, displaying a fan of burner phones, identical to the one Bones was holding. "I followed a trail of bread crumbs."

Dragomirov laughed and then returned both his attention and the aimpoint of his weapon to Maddock. "So much for your precautions."

Maddock managed, with an effort, to maintain his confidently neutral expression, but his heart was a trip hammer in his chest. "Corey still knows we're down here."

"It will be my word against his." The mobster shifted into a shooting stance, a sure sign that there would be no further negotiations.

"Wait!" Maddock threw up his arms in what must have looked like an attempt to plead, but then glanced over at Bones and nodded his head toward the arched opening behind them. "Fall back," he whispered from the corner of his mouth.

Bones didn't question the directive, but raised his hands in imitation of Maddock's stance, and slid back a step. "Max," he murmured. "Stay with me."

Dragomirov, perhaps misinterpreting the exchange,

frowned. "You didn't strike me as someone who would beg at the end. I'm almost disappointed. Maybe we do this old-fashioned way. Kneel and put your hands behind your head."

Maddock slid back a step. Bones and Riddle were right behind him, almost inside the arched passage leading nowhere. "I'm not going to do that," he said, striving for a tone of calm assuredness. "And if I were you, I'd be very careful about where you point that gun right now. If you shoot and miss me, there's a good chance your bullet will smash through the flowstone behind us... Flood this whole place with boiling water. Good luck getting your treasure after that."

Dragomirov, clearly unimpressed with the warning, took a step forward. "Then I had better not miss."

Maddock moved as well. "Fall back, fall back," he muttered, keeping his eyes on the pistol as he retreated through the opening.

Bones and Riddle had gotten the message, scrambling back into the narrow dead-end corridor. Maddock could hear the crunch of their feet on the thin layer of travertine covering the floor.

Dragomirov kept advancing. Maddock took a little comfort in the fact that the mobster hadn't fired yet, but he knew the standoff wouldn't last.

Krasimir came alongside his brother, whirling his butterfly knife back and forth in what was surely meant to be an intimidating display of expertise. "No need to take chances, brother. Let me handle it."

Dragomirov appeared to be considering the request, so Maddock took advantage of the moment to draw the only thing he had that might work as a weapon—his pry bar. Krasimir hesitated, evidently unprepared for any show of resistance, but Maddock had no intention of getting into a knife fight with the young *mutri*, not while Dragomirov still held a gun on them. He had other plans for the pry bar.

He continued backing up until he both felt and heard the flowstone beneath his boots. Gripping the length of metal in both hands, he raised the pry bar across his body and drove the chisel tip into the white flowstone.

The effect on the two mobsters was everything Maddock could have hoped for. Both men backpedaled away from the opening as if they thought Maddock was trying to open a doorway to Hell itself. But aside from sending a jarring impact up his forearms and knocking loose a scattering of crystal fragments, the blow seemed to have little real effect.

So he tried again.

The second blow dislodged a piece of travertine the size of a dinner plate, exposing wet brick underneath.

"Fool," Dragomirov snarled. "What will that accomplish? You'll kill us all."

"I can live with that," Maddock said, and drove the pry bar into a wet mortar joint.

Dark cracks spread out from the point of impact, tracing around the individual bricks. Fat beads of moisture oozed from the fissures, and began dribbling down the wall.

Krasimir said something urgent in Bulgarian—probably "shoot him"—but Dragomirov only nodded his head, and continued retreating until he was barely visible through the archway. "You'll never make it out of here," he shouted, and then he was swallowed up completely by the darkness.

Maddock sagged in relief at the apparent reprieve.

"Damn," Bones said slowly. "I'll deny saying it, but I'm a little turned on right now."

Riddle made a choking sound that might have been a laugh. "Deny it all you want, but the cameras are still rolling. They are still rolling, aren't they? Because *that* was some frigging amazing television. I thought he was gonna call your bluff."

"What bluff?" Maddock said, his voice almost deserting him. "Come on. Let's get out of here."

"You know they're going to be waiting for us."

"Maybe. Corey knows we're down here and he knows what to do if we don't come out. We've got time on our side."

Suddenly, a hissing jet of water and steam erupted from the wall, right at the point where Maddock had struck it. He jumped back as the mini-geyser shot completely across the narrow passage to splash against the opposite wall.

"You were saying?" Bones had to shout to be heard over the rushing sound.

The sustained outpouring of water caused more pieces of mortar to crumble away, increasing the flow, and further hastening the wall's destruction. Meanwhile, the torrent was spreading across the floor, rolling out in an ever-expanding puddle. One leading edge had crawled onto the thin layer of flowstone on which Maddock stood, to lap at his boot soles. Close to the source, it was already an inch deep.

"Blow through," Bones urged, coming alongside Maddock.

But Maddock threw out a hand to block him. "No."

"If we don't get moving, our only way out is going to be flooded."

As if to punctuate the warning, an entire brick tore loose from the wall. The breach intensified the volume of discharge, taking it from a mere jet of water to something like the blast from a firehose. The brick was hurled across the passage, striking the opposite wall as if it had been shot from a cannon. The other kind of volume—the kind measured in decibels—increased as well. The close quarters amplified the noise to near-deafening levels.

Bones put his mouth close to Maddock's ear. "Our coveralls will give us some protection, but if we don't go now—"

Maddock shook his head. "No! Push back!"

He used his outstretched arm to shepherd Bones back a step. The big man's incredulity was palpable, but he did not resist. Their retreat brought them to an anxious Riddle, who unlike Bones, did not seem especially eager to run the gauntlet.

The water was now ankle deep and rising fast. Maddock could feel the heat seeping through the leather. It was hot, but definitely nowhere near boiling. More like stepping into a Jacuzzi than a simmering stewpot. Part of this, he guessed, was due to the fact that immediately upon contact with the air, the water began giving up some of its stored heat, but Maddock suspected—or more accurately, *prayed*—that was only a partial explanation. If he was wrong….

"Please tell me you've got some kind of crazy plan to get us out of this," Riddle shouted.

"A sane plan would be preferable," Bones put in, "but I know you better than that."

Before Maddock could even attempt to articulate what he had in mind, a huge section of the wall—about four feet square—broke loose, vomiting out an equally huge cascade. The initial splash showered the three men with hot droplets, and sent out waves that reached mid-thigh on Maddock. The sudden immersion triggered a sympathetic reaction throughout his body. His pulse skyrocketed, as his autonomic nervous system sought to cool itself by rapid circulation of blood. He clenched his teeth but could not entirely suppress a low wail of pain.

And yet, through it all, the rational part of his brain was offering quiet reassurance.

This isn't so bad. I've taken hotter showers. It's just the suddenness of it.

After only a few seconds of exposure, the initial discomfort passed, but his heart continued to pound away in a futile effort to dissipate the heat. While they wouldn't boil to death, prolonged exposure would eventually have harmful and possibly fatal consequences.

"I hope that... plan of yours... didn't involve...going out the...way we came in," said Bones. The words came out in hitching gasps as he fought to catch his breath. "Because... it's underwater now."

Maddock shook his head and pointed to the hole through which hot water now poured like a waterfall. "That's... our way... out."

Bones stared at him as if he had just suggested asking Scotty to beam them back to the Starship Enterprise. Maddock didn't have the words, much less the breath, to explain. It really was a crazy plan, and it hinged upon a lot of half-baked—or was it soft-boiled?—assumptions. If even one of those was wrong, their collective goose would literally be cooked.

His first assumption was that whomever had walled off the passage to seal in the treasure had also diverted a hot spring to create an additional barrier to entry. The volume of water rushing out of the breach in the wall seemed to confirm that this was true. The second assumption, which followed naturally, was that breaking through the wall—just as Riddle had earlier suggested—would lead to an exit.

As his earlier reasons for dismissing the idea were no longer relevant, he hoped to hell that there really was a way out on the other side of the wall.

The third assumption, and perhaps the most critical, was that they could endure the hot tub from hell long enough to reach that mythical exit.

The rush of water continued to erode the hole, but as the water came level with the breach, the fury of the outpouring was muted considerably. Maddock and the others could only stand by and let the waters rise. Waist high... Chest high... And then, just at it seemed they would have to begin swimming in the hot bath, the top of the hole was covered completely.

An eerie stillness filled what little air remained.

Maddock pushed against the current to approach the opening. Below the surface, he could feel the water rushing out of the hole, and knew it would continue to do so for a while longer, at least until the water table equalized on both sides, but with the hole completely covered, the fury of the outflow was greatly reduced. He was able to find the opening with an outstretched hand, gripping the exposed brick.

"Swim through," he said, and then closed his eyes tight and plunged his head into the water.

Because his body had sufficiently acclimated to the heat, full submersion brought little additional discomfort. With his heart rate still elevated however, he knew his lung capacity would be severely diminished. If he didn't find the surface in about thirty seconds, he probably wouldn't find it at all.

As soon as he was through and on the other side, he began feeling his way up the wall. The brick was rough against his gloved fingertips. After a few seconds, he could feel the wall curving into a round, vaulted ceiling, just like the passage behind.

If his heart had not already been pounding, it might have skipped a beat. He had bet everything on the hope that the passage on the other side of the wall would have drained enough to create a pocket of breathable air.

Bet everything, and lost....

21

Dragomirov's plan had been to lie in ambush at the top of the descending passage, just past the spot where Maddock had broken through the brick to reveal the tunnel to the treasure vault, but before he and Krasimir could reach it, a rush of hot, humid air from below told him that it would no longer be necessary.

By foolishly breaking through the wall, flooding the subterranean vault with superheated water, Maddock had signed his own death warrant. Dragomirov didn't think the water would rise as high as the hypocaust ducts, but it seemed prudent not to find out firsthand.

A few seconds later, he reached the opening Maddock had created. A neat pile of bricks partially blocked the passage to his immediate right, providing a tacit reminder that they needed to continue straight.

Yet, as he crawled along, a sliver of doubt wormed into his brain. "Is this right?" he asked.

"What?" Krasimir's reply was muffled, indistinct.

"Are we going the right way?" Dragomirov said, almost shouting to be heard.

Krasimir was silent for several seconds before finally admitting the truth. "I don't know. I wasn't paying attention."

Dragomirov muttered an oath, but he couldn't fault his brother. He too had failed to make note of the route. Still, as long as the passage didn't flood, they ought to be able to figure it out through trial and error.

The duct bent to the left, then a short ways further on, hooked to the right. The sliver of doubt continued to worry deeper into his consciousness.

Wrong way. Wrong way. You're lost. Turn back before it's too late.

"No," he whispered. "This is the right way."

And he was almost sure that it was. The air on his face felt cooler, didn't it?

He stopped as a new problem presented itself—a four-way intersection. *I remember this,* he thought, but then the doubting voice challenged him. *Are you sure? There must be dozens of intersections like this. Maddock called it a maze.*

"Go straight," Krasimir called from behind him. "I remember this. We're almost there."

The admonition silenced the voice of doubt. With renewed urgency, Dragomirov belly crawled forward, emerging at last into the open space beneath the church floor. Directly ahead, a glowing square marked the location of the trapdoor leading up into the church.

His concerns about being lost underground were swept entirely away, replaced instead by a feeling of triumph.

He had won. Maddock was surely dead. Samuil's treasure would be his, alone. He would have to find a way to retrieve it, but that was merely an academic problem. Just knowing that it was real was enough.

With renewed vigor, he scuttled toward the trapdoor, thrusting head and shoulders up through, and quickly scrambled up and out of the hole like someone escaping from a premature burial. He rolled away from the opening, lay on his back, staring up at the painted icons on the domed ceiling, and began to laugh.

Corey's first hint of trouble came when the feed from Maddock's GoPro abruptly froze, displaying the all too familiar throbber.

Connecting… Connecting….

He and Slava had been following the subterranean exploration remotely from the relative safety of a table inside the McDonalds just down the street from the cordoned area, while alternately monitoring the situation with the bogus gas leak alarm Slava had triggered.

Everything had gone off exactly according to plan.

Right up until the moment when it didn't.

One moment, the tablet screen showed Maddock walking slowly through an unbelievable hoard of golden treasure, and the next… Nothing.

Corey did not panic, as he had the previous night when his friends had gone into the vault at the museum, but waited patiently for the connection to be restored. Maddock had probably moved too far from the last repeater.

"Bones," he called out. "You need to activate another burner phone."

Although Maddock was the only one outfitted with a GoPro, both he and Bones had Bluetooth earbuds. Even if Maddock was out of range, Bones might not be.

But after several more seconds of silence, Corey had to admit that he had lost contact with Bones as well.

Still, there was no reason to freak out. Maddock and Bones could handle themselves.

"Something's wrong," Slava announced, bursting Corey's fragile bubble of optimism.

He gave a helpless shrug. "We knew there was a chance the repeaters wouldn't do the trick."

Slava continued to frown. "Go to the drone feed."

Corey tapped the screen and brought up the live

video from the still hovering drone. It showed the exterior of the old church in the courtyard behind the Largo Complex. For all the activity, or rather the lack of it, they might have been looking at a still image.

"Back it up," Slava said.

Corey gave her a questioning look, which she seemed to completely ignore, and then did as instructed, pausing the live feed and rewinding the recorded footage, first at 2X speed, then 4X. The image on the screen did not change however, and if not for the progress bar at the bottom of the screen, slowly shifting from right to left, it would not have been apparent that anything was happening.

But then something flickered in and out of existence.

"There," Slava cried out, even as Corey paused the rewind and started normal playback.

Nothing happened for a few seconds, but then a vaguely man-shaped figure shuffled into view, moving directly toward the church doors.

"Is that a fireman?" Corey asked, and then as the man pushed through the doors and entered the church, added, "What's he doing? Do you think he found them?"

Slava's head bobbed once. "I don't think he's a real fire fighter," she said. "I think it is one of Dragomirov's men."

Corey decided maybe a little bit of panic was warranted, but Slava remained cool and collected as she took out her phone and dialed a number. Maddock had left explicit instructions about what to do if things went sideways, and this definitely met that threshold.

Corey switched back to the drone's live feed, watching and praying that Maddock, Bones and Riddle would emerge, but as before, the image on screen remained maddeningly unchanged. Corey tried calling

Bones' number, but was immediately informed that the caller was unavailable and no voice mailbox had been set up.

Nearly ten minutes passed before uniformed police officers swarmed into view, advancing toward the old church with guns drawn. Half a dozen of them lined up beside the door and executed a tactical entry, while the rest remained outside, evidently awaiting further instructions.

Five more minutes ticked slowly by, and then the doors to the church swung open. A police officer emerged, and then another, but the second man was escorting a handcuffed Boyan Dragomirov. Close behind them was another shackled suspect. Though he still wore the heavy black turnout gear of a fire fighter, the man's helmet had been removed to reveal his identity—Krasimir Dragomirov. A couple more officers followed, the last of whom closed the doors before trailing after his comrades.

Corey kept watching… Kept waiting… But nobody else came out of the church. He pounded his fist on the table in impotent frustration. "Where are they?"

22

Just as hope began to desert him, Maddock broke through the surface with a splash, and felt warm air on his face.

He opened his eyes and saw the curved barrel-vault of the ceiling, mere inches from his nose. As he blew out the breath he had been holding, he became aware of strange oscillation—part sound, part sensation—filling both the air and the water surrounding him. It was, he realized, the same hum they had heard earlier in the treasure chamber, but now, closer to the source, he could tell that it wasn't merely the product of water rushing through a subterranean channel. There was a rhythm to it—a mechanical rhythm that he recognized.

As he shone his light back and forth, searching for the source, he saw two more lights glowing in the murk below. A moment later, Bones' head emerged, followed a second or two later by Riddle. The latter was panting heavily, his face bright red.

"All right, Maddock," Bones said, only a little less breathlessly. "So far, so good. Now what?"

Maddock shushed him. "Listen. Do you hear it?"

Bones returned a frown, but did as directed. His frown quickly gave way to a hopeful grin. "That's a pump."

Maddock nodded, and continued trying to get a fix on the source. After a few more seconds, he pointed in what he thought was the right direction. "That way," he said, and began kicking his legs to propel him down the length of the passage.

The noise grew louder as he moved, a sure sign that he had chosen correctly. As he rounded a bend, he spied something protruding from the ceiling to disappear into the water below. It looked like a thin vertical support column, but as he got closer, he realized that it was actually a large-bore pipe. It was also the source of the vibration.

He eagerly swam toward the pipe, and upon reaching it, saw that it continued up the side of a much larger vertical shaft. Opposite the pipe, a ladder of iron rungs, spaced about twelve inches apart, ran up the curved interior of the shaft.

Maddock snagged the lowest rung and easily pulled himself up high enough to reach the next rung. As more of his body came out of the water, the amount of effort required to lift himself higher increased proportionately. Under normal conditions, he would have been able to pull himself all the way up with arm strength alone, but prolonged immersion had sapped his energy, leaving him dangerously depleted. With his lower torso still underwater, it was all he could do to heave himself up to the next rung. Summoning what felt like the last of his strength, he kicked his legs hard, propelling himself up out of the water, and made a dynamic leap up two more rungs—high enough to get his right foot on the lowest rung.

Just being out of the hot water was enough to restore a measure of vital energy. He resumed climbing, letting his legs do most of the work, and soon reached the top of the shaft. Not surprisingly, it was covered with a heavy iron plate.

He climbed higher, bending over at the waist in order to put his back against the plate, then flexed his legs and pushed.

The plate refused to budge.

Below, Bones had somehow managed to help Riddle

pull himself up out of the water. The effort had cost him dearly. While Riddle now hung a few rungs below Maddock, well out of the water, Bones was hanging from the bottom rung, still partly submerged, and panting heavily. When he caught Maddock's eye, he growled, "Either open the damn thing, or get out of the way and let a man do it."

Maddock doubted that Bones had enough strength left to even make the climb, never mind pushing away the cover. Nevertheless, the taunt spurred him to try again, not because the words stung, but because if he didn't succeed in getting the cover off, Bones might very well die.

He blew out his breath in a torrent of curses, then drew in another and tried again, straining until stars began to flitter before his eyes. A howl tore from his throat, but the plate did not move an inch….

And then it did.

Though he could hardly believe it, the heavy metal covering had risen a couple inches. Even more incredibly, it was moving laterally, sliding out of the way. A crescent-shaped opening appeared above him, waxing like the moon as the plate continued moving. In that newly revealed gap, Maddock saw faces staring down at him… Staring out from under helmets like the one Krasimir had been wearing.

Firefighters.

But unlike Krasimir, these men were not imposters.

This was a rescue.

Multiple hands reached down into the hole and lifted him up, gently but urgently bearing him away. He realized only as he was carried through a door leading outside, that they had come up inside a small pump house, situated next to a brick-paved plaza. Occupying the plaza were several low, red-and-white striped walls, outfitted with metal spigots that spewed out unending streams of naturally-heated mineral water.

Maddock was carried past these to a waiting ambulance, where paramedics immediately went to work assessing him. He was already feeling a lot better, but knew better than to reject their ministrations. Once he was sure that his friends had been likewise rescued, he lay back and let the medics do their job. Riddle was groggy and the medics started an I.V. but Bones was already coming around.

"Dane! Bones!"

Maddock looked around for the source of the voice and spotted Corey and Slava, waving like ecstatic children at a carnival. They hurried over, stopping short only when one of the paramedics raised a hand, warning them to keep their distance.

"Thank God, they found you," Corey said.

Maddock nodded, dully, but then some of the pieces fell into place. "Maybe we should be thanking you," he said. "How did you find us?"

Corey's cheeks reddened a little and he looked away, sheepishly, but Slava was quick to fill in the gaps. "When you got close to the surface, we were able to connect with your GoPro."

"The feed is GPS tagged, so we knew exactly where to look for you."

"Must have had a hell of time convincing them," Bones muttered.

"Not really," replied Slava. "Not when we were able to show them Samuil's treasure." She flashed a triumphant grin. "You are heroes of Bulgaria now."

"Even though we had to flood the place to keep Dragomirov from killing us?" asked Bones.

"They weren't happy about that," Corey admitted.

"But at least the treasure is safe from looters now."

"What about Dragomirov?" asked Maddock.

"They caught him and his brother before they made it out of the church," replied Slava. "They have been arrested for kidnapping and murder."

"Murder?"

"Krasimir killed a firefighter and took his gear to sneak into the restricted area. He was still wearing it when they caught him."

"I'm betting his friends in the government won't be able to help him beat that rap."

"Not with video evidence of him holding you at gunpoint."

Maddock breathed a sigh of relief. "Hopefully that will help when we have to explain why we faked the gas leak, not to mention breaking into the museum to steal Krum's Cup."

She nodded. "Don't worry. Like I said, You are national heroes."

"And as Max would say," Corey added, "You made some friggin' amazing TV."

Maddock could only chuckle. "Great. I can die happy now."

"I'll die happy if I never see another hot tub," Bones grumbled.

Maddock laughed. "Even if it's full of bikini models?"

Bones pondered this for a moment, then shrugged. "You're right. I'm over it."

EPILOGUE

The real national hero, as it turned out, was Dmitri Marinov. At Maddock's urging, he went back to his original story of seeing Vulchan Voivode in a dream, and in so doing, threw a little shade on Rumen Nikolov, who had been quick to claim a key role in leading Maddock and his friends to Samuil's treasure. When asked to comment on Nikolov's claims, Marinov rolled his eyes. "If they had listened to me, they would have found the treasure twenty years ago."

A careful review of Maddock's GoPro footage allowed the government-sponsored archaeological team to determine the easiest route into the treasure vault. Rather than send divers into the geothermally-heated water, they elected to simply excavate a new passage down into it. This necessitated closing the street to the north of the Largo Complex, but compared to the original Tsarichina excavation, the recovery of Samuil's gold posed little technical challenge.

A team of archaeologists and cave explorers from the Peter Tranteev Society were dispatched to Tsarichina to retrieve the small cache of gold coins there and begin the search for the original entrance that Vuchan might have used to access the cave.

Corey and Riddle spent the following two days sequestered in Corey's room, reviewing the mountain of raw footage and cutting it together into something that Riddle could take to the networks.

Bones spent most of that time in the casino, declaring that their discoveries and subsequent escape from

Dragomirov and the flooded tunnel indicated that Lady Luck was presently smiling on him.

Slava offered to take Maddock on a walking tour of the Serdica Ruins and other historical sites. He did not get the sense that she was interested in a romantic liaison so much as a distraction from her life, which suited him just fine.

On the second day, they drove east, to the city of Plovdiv, and on to Bulgaria's famed Rose Valley. It was not the sort of place he would normally have chosen as a vacation destination, but after the events of the preceding days, he welcomed a chance to literally stop and smell the roses.

On the drive back, he broached the subject he sensed she had been avoiding. "So what's next for you?"

She did not answer right away, but continued to stare straight ahead. Finally, she said, "That's what I am trying to figure out. For years, all I cared about was exposing Rumen Nikolov as a fraud. That didn't quite go according to plan, thanks to you—"

"You're welcome."

She looked over at him, and frowned. "I put Max in danger. I put all of you in danger. And that fire fighter who was killed. That was my fault."

"No," Maddock said. "Not that. Some of what you say is true, but you aren't to blame for that."

His assertion did not appear to relieve her guilt, so he went on. "But if you really feel that way, then do something about it."

"What?"

"Whether or not you intended to, you did help take down Dragomirov. Maybe there's more Atanas the hacker can do to fight organized crime."

"Maybe," Slava said, and shook her head once.

Maddock had to once more remind himself that this was a signal of affirmation. She would at least consider the suggestion.

As they were nearing Sofia, Riddle sent Maddock a text message.

Have some great news. Meet for drinks downstairs?

Maddock replied back that they were still on the road, and suggested postponing the rendezvous an hour.

At the appointed time, they joined Bones, Corey and Riddle in the casino lounge. Riddle looked about ready to burst with excitement.

"So, I sent our rough cut to my agent, who absolutely loved it. He's going to shop it to all the major streaming services. Somebody is definitely going to pick this up. He thinks we're going to have a bidding war for it."

"That's great news," Maddock said.

"So I can count on you then?"

"Count on me?"

"We're still polishing the pitch," Riddle went on, as if he hadn't heard the question, "but I've already got a kick-ass title for it. 'Destination: Adventure.' What do you think? Pretty catchy."

"What did you mean by 'count on' me?" Maddock pressed.

"Well, all of you," answered Riddle, gesturing to include Bones and Corey. "I want you guys to co-host the show with me. I'll do the exposition stuff—explain the myths and mysteries. You guys can handle the adventure part."

Maddock sighed. "Max, we've gone over this. We're not interested in being in your show." He glanced over at Bones, and then amended, "Well, I'm not. I have a job, and it keeps me plenty busy."

"But that's just it. You'll just keep doing what you do. The only difference is, we'll be filming it all. And this wouldn't even be a full-time gig. We're talking ten… maybe, twelve episodes, per season. Some of those would be two-parters. It's a win-win."

Maddock rubbed the bridge of his nose as if trying to soothe a headache. "Look, I know it must seem like what we do is non-stop excitement, but honestly, most of the time it's pretty boring stuff."

"Really?" Bones said. "Because that's not how I remember things."

"How about this," pressed Riddle. "Let me tag along with you guys for a while and see what shakes out."

Maddock sighed again. "I don't know—"

"I've already figured out what we can do next. There's a ton of really weird stuff right here in Bulgaria. There's Devil's Throat Cave… We've gotta check that out. But I really want to look into the Rhodope Skull."

Bones shifted forward, clearly interested. "Another skull. Is this one a soup bowl?"

"Researchers think it might have been the skull of an extraterrestrial, though one Bulgarian psychic believes it was a failed science experiment conducted by the Atlanteans. No one knows for sure because shortly after it was discovered in the Rhodope Mountains, south of here, it disappeared."

As Riddle went on, describing in great detail the history and controversy surrounding the possibly alien skull, Maddock could see that the others had already fallen under Riddle's spell. He laughed, gave a small shake of his head, and flagged down a passing waiter to order a beer."

Bones glanced at him and quirked an eyebrow. "What's up?"

"Nothing, really," Maddock said. "But I guess I know where I'm gonna be tomorrow."

The End

About the Authors

David Wood is the USA Today bestselling author of the Dane Maddock Adventures and several other books and series. He also writes fantasy under the pen name David Debord. He's a member of International Thriller Writers and the Horror Writers Association, and also reviews for New York Journal of Books. Learn more about his work at http://www.davidwoodweb.comor drop by and say hello on Facebook at www.facebook.com/davidwoodbooks.

Sean Ellis has authored and co-authored more than two dozen action-adventure novels, including the Nick Kismet adventures, the Jack Sigler/Chess Team series with Jeremy Robinson, and the Jade Ihara adventures with David Wood. He served with the Army National Guard in Afghanistan, and has a Bachelor of Science degree in Natural Resources Policy from Oregon State University. Sean is also a member of the International Thriller Writers organization. He currently resides in Arizona, where he divides his time between writing, adventure sports, and trying to figure out how to save the world. Learn more about Sean at seanellisauthor.com

Made in the USA
Middletown, DE
14 February 2020